The Vineyard

and other Stories

Wanda Fries

ISBN-13: 978-0615638225
ISBN-10: 0615638228

Acknowledgements

Most of the short stories in this collection have appeared in other publications. "Mel's Back" was first published in 1989 in *The Michigan Quarterly Review* and was later reprinted in *Writers & Their Craft,* Wayne State University Press, 1991. "The Vineyard" appeared in *drafthorse,* Winter, 2013. "The Baby" (with the title "Rags") was first published in *Appalachian Heritage* in 1987.

"Fault Lines" appeared in *New Growth: New Kentucky Writings* in 2007. "Working Sketches" was published in *River City Review* in 1989 and "Houses" the same year in *Special Report: Fiction.* "Drug Therapy" was published in the *Mid-Atlantic Review* in 2003. "Fault Lines" won an honorable mention in the Appalachian Writers Association Harriette Arnow Short Story Prize and "The Vineyard" won first prize in the Carnegie Center (Lexington) Short Story Contest.

This book is dedicated to my long-time friend and fellow writer and traveler, Betty Peterson, who has been my unfailing supporter and sister of the soul since we met in 1988.

The Stories

The Vineyard

Mornings Dr. Wyatt stands barefoot in his kitchen, watching the sun rise over his vineyard. The grape vines stretch, row upon row, into the distance as far as he can see.

The vineyard is the folly of Wyatt's late middle age, and he has spent a fortune on it and the small winery he intends to have up and running within the next three years. As a doctor, he has never had any interest in growing tobacco. An oncologist, he sees death daily, in small, incremental doses. But when an extension agent told him that some of the first vineyards and wineries in the country were in Kentucky, he visited a couple of them in the northern part of the state and was hooked on the idea.

Now his walkout basement is full of gleaming stainless steel casks and other equipment, including a wine press from Italy and pruning shears from a kibbutz near Jerusalem. What better way to spend his money than on the grapes that unfurl their leaves in spring, sending tendrils to wind around the wires he has stretched in straight rows, anchored with wood crosspieces, for the vines to cling to?

He loves everything about the process. First, he breaks up the rich dirt with his tiller, and then he digs holes for the new plants. He digs and digs, and then he stands, leaning on the shovel handle, watching the sunset bathe the vineyard in coral light. Today is the first day of harvest, when, after three years of pruning and shaping the vines, of cutting off the grape clusters to force the plant's energy into the roots, he has a sizeable crop of grapes to harvest, enough to make his first batch of wine from his own grapes.

To harvest the grapes, he has invited his friends from town, who feel it is romantic to be a part of the enterprise. Tonight, they will pick the grapes and then feed the clusters into a machine that separates the berries from the stems. Then Wyatt will scoop the blue fruit pulp into the stainless steel casks to ferment.

His friends Vic and Stacy work the rows nearest the road. Vic, Wyatt's friend and tax attorney, calls out from a row over from Wyatt, yelling like a startled cat. Wyatt hears the two of them discussing whether Vic was stung by a yellow jacket or a bumblebee. Wyatt has vials of medicine for stings, and he sends to the house for them, pretending to be sympathetic. But what he really feels is superiority. He likes the bees that hum languidly among his vines, under the cloak of leaves, to drink the nectar of his grapes, for they are hungry and alive. He is man enough to enjoy nature beyond the confines of a houseboat or a golf cart or a screened-in porch. On this patch of ground, just as in the hospital where he faces death every day, he is still a man.

Tonight he should be ecstatic, but he is distant and distracted, waiting for Anna, the girl who, for the past year, has been working in his office. She promised to come and pick grapes, drink wine, and celebrate with him—and his wife, of course—their first real harvest. Although Anna is still a girl, from his perspective, not more than twenty-five or so, she already has two small children and is on her own, the father having left without a forwarding address. His office manager gave Anna a job on the spot because of her intelligence and potential. Later, when Anna faced eviction from her apartment because she couldn't pay the rent, Wyatt, as he has done for so many people, came to the rescue. He fixed up a small rental house he owns and let her move in rent-free with her children until she could get back on her feet.

Anna has warm brown eyes and a black braid that tumbles down her back nearly to her waist. This spring, to repay Wyatt for his kindness, she helped him divide the perennials in the large flower garden to the left of the house. Wyatt watched a bee clean its forelegs on her smooth brown arms while she stood still in wonder and watched it, unafraid, waiting patiently for it to fly away. He longed to be the bee, and he longed to be Anna, in that strange dance of her extended arm and the bee taking salt and sweat from her skin.

Anna is the lowest of his office assistants, but he started her off from the very first day at the same salary he pays the woman who has been there for six years. After two or three months, Belinda, the office manager, a middle-aged woman with perfectly arranged blonde hair to match the perfection of her job performance, came into Wyatt's office to tell him he was causing dissension in the ranks. She shook a little with the nervousness she felt at confronting him, but he let her finish without saying a word.

Then, leaning across the desk, he asked, "Why is this so important? Are any of you unhappy with what I pay you?"

No, she shakes her head, no. Everyone who works for Dr. Wyatt knows he is a good and generous man, who pays his office and nursing staff better than any other doctor in town does. He often takes care of their relatives who have cancer. At the end of the treatment, whether the end is death, defeat, or healing, he nearly always writes on the bill "paid in full" in gratitude for his employee's service and pity for the sorrow and misfortune they and their loved ones have endured.

"We go to church together," he reminds Belinda. "Try to remember that Anna is a single mother. She's trying to work, raise children, and study to be a nurse, all at the same time. She works hard here, and she does a good job. Why should it bother anyone that I choose to try and help her?"

Perhaps they object to her salary because they suspect the truth, that Wyatt is in love with her. He tries to love her prudently, like a father. Only once in thirty years of marriage to a woman he loves—a lovely woman who has been good to him, a partner and a friend—has he been unfaithful, and the experience was so awful, the guilt so profound, that he was never tempted to repeat it.

But at the office, he waits for Belinda to be preoccupied with work so that he can make his furtive offerings. He does not give Anna anything she will feel compelled to refuse. He keeps it simple—a book he read and liked, a mug with an inspirational saying, or a small blue bowl for her paper clips. Not once has he even suggested anything inappropriate, though when he comes into the office after making his rounds and stands at the counter filling out the charts between patients, he searches her out. He lets his eyes rest on the braid that falls between her narrow shoulders or on her small white teeth as she studies the form printing from the computer and gnaws the end of her pen.

Wyatt is still handsome in his silvery affluence, his skin darkened from the sun and his body lean from the exercise of farming. In his waking hours, he has no ulterior motives for his kindness to Anna, but often he wakes feverish from sleep, dreaming of Anna in ways that he would not tell anyone and blushes to remember. He dreams of her mouth open and red as new wine, her long brown arms looped around his waist. After their kisses, he watches with wonder as she loosens her braid, letting her hair tumble in waves down her narrow back.

Tonight, he listens, distracted, to the banter of the dozen or so friends who are here helping him. In the cooler that holds bottled water, he has saved a wild rose picked from among the briars that choke the fence-line at the perimeter of his property.

Anna comes, finally, at seven, wearing blue jeans and a denim shirt with the sleeves rolled up. Her long dark braid swings like a bell rope across the V of her back. The teenage boys stop cutting the clusters of grapes to watch her, and his friend Vic, nursing his stung finger in his mouth, looks over at Wyatt with a foolish grin and his eyebrows raised. Where have you been hiding her?

Wyatt hands her a pair of pruning shears. Oblivious to the stir she has caused, Anna concentrates on cutting the clusters of grapes, tossing them with a plop into the crate beside her. When she has worked for an hour, Wyatt takes her the rose. She turns to him, smiling, and Wyatt winds the stem into her hair. She is a quiet girl, and he doesn't expect her to speak. Her smile is enough. But this time, to his wonder and dismay, she lifts her chin and gives him a kiss, soft as bee wings, upon his cheek. He bows like a lover and leaves her. He loves her, and he could be her lover. Why shouldn't he?

Feverish, he picks row upon row of the remaining grapes, each one plump and ripe, ready for harvesting, and all the time seeing her in front of him, imagining her arms locked around him, her body naked and open, curving to his, dreaming of her eyes. When he has finished the fifth row, he goes to find her. But when he catches sight of her, halfway down the last row, he sees that Simon, Vic's son, in his twenties and home from graduate school, has gotten there first. Simon has come by the office a couple of times to take Anna to lunch, but until now, Wyatt, busy with patients, has not paid any attention.

Wyatt stands at the end of the row, his nerves thrumming, and watches Simon hold a cluster of grapes to Anna's mouth. With familiar intimacy, she rests her hand on Simon's hip. She bites one, two, three grapes, and then offers them back to Simon from her mouth. Simon leans forward to take them, touching her tongue with his. He puts his arm around her and pulls her against him, his hand tracing the line of her chin and moving down, softly and quickly, to her waist.

Wyatt watches. In the early September evening, as the bees drink the last sweetness from the few grapes left upon the vines the lovers kiss,. Wyatt's groin stirs, but it is not simply Anna's body he desires, perhaps not even Anna, but some part of himself that he has lost. He wants to be himself, Wyatt, but young again like Simon, ready to save the broken and injured souls who will put themselves into his healing hands. But he is not young, and he knows the weight of sorrow that comes from learning that everyone he touches, no matter what his skill, sooner or later will die.

He sighs and his heart breaks. In the softness of the falling twilight, the breeze sighs with him, and above the gabled roof of his house, the moon rocks back, resting against the violet sky.

From behind, Wyatt hears someone coming, and, in one more act of generosity to this woman whom he loves, loves at last as he should, he puts his arm around Vic's shoulders and turns Vic away from what they should not see. He shares a joke he heard at the hospital. Vic laughs, and they walk to the patio where the grapes will be de-stemmed, pressed, and casked. Wyatt's wife walks across the lawn smiling. He kisses her cheek lightly and takes the glass of wine from her hand.

He glances back, just once, across his shoulder. Simon and Anna emerge from the tangle of vines. Simon laughs and pulls Anna close, and Wyatt's white rose falls. frayed and already wilting, to the dry September ground.

Mel's Back

Mel has just turned off the shower when he hears Evelyn rattling in the kitchen. He slides the glass door open, stepping onto the bath mat. With the heel of his hand, he wipes a circle in the steam on the mirror. He slept last night in the cab of his semi. The hot water has eased the stiffness from his joints, erased the grit from his face. While he shaves, the scent of bacon tracks him down the narrow hall.

Evelyn smiles as he comes barefoot into the kitchen. He's naked from the waist up, the hair on his chest still damp. He drapes a pink towel across the back of a dinette chair, and, turning it to face him, straddles it, folding his arms across the back.

"Hello, stranger," she says, striking a can of biscuits against the edge of the counter to pop it open. He used to tease her, telling her she made canned biscuits just like his mother used to make. "What brings you through this time?"

"Got a load of lumber to haul to Neon. Got in around two."

She's used to him dropping in. He got into the habit while their sons were still at home. But even now that both boys are grown up and gone, he still rolls in every few months to see how she is. Besides, it's easier for the boys to stay in contact with her. At least that makes a nice excuse.

Books and papers clutter the table. At forty, Evelyn has gone back to college, to Lexington Theological Seminary for a divinity degree. ("Don't surprise me none," Mel's mother said when she heard. "Scratch most any preacher around here, and you find somebody who used to be a drunk.") A red-bound book called *Strategies in Counseling* lies open on page seventy. When Mel picks it up, he sees notes scattered down the margin in Evelyn's looping hand.

He lays the book face down. "How's school?"

"It's all right." She dumps frozen orange juice into a plastic pitcher. Her hands are big and brown, the nails chewed into the quicks. "I'm tired of doing fourteen things at once, but I ought to finish next year. That big church they're building out on the bypass?"

"The one that looks like Six Flags over Jesus?"

She laughs. "That very one. I've been working out there part time as a youth minister. They may put me on full-time, when I get my degree. You ought not to make fun of it. Lots of people find their way in that church when they've tried everything else."

He doesn't know what to say to that, so he doesn't say anything.

On the ledge at the base of the window, Evelyn's grey-striped tomcat sleeps in the sun. Mel gets up to scratch it behind the ears, but when he touches it, it arches its back and leaps down. "I can't believe how built up it is out here," he says, looking out the window at the trailers that stud what used to be pastureland. Their white metal siding glitters like cheap jewelry in a green felt case. "The whole county, really. It's a lot different from when we were growing up."

He takes a fork and wiggles bacon around in the pan. Over the sizzle of grease, he asks her if she's heard from the boys.

"Wayne called last week. He got hired temporary at Toyota,

over at Georgetown. Good money, if it works into anything permanent."

"Ben?"

"He's re-enlisted. I'm afraid to turn the news on. They're shipping everybody they can find to Iraq or Afghanistan. I wish he'd have just come on home."

"And do what? Face it, Evelyn. We never could do a thing with him. Army's the only thing he could have done. He needs the discipline. Anyway, I've got a lot of time on the road to think, and I've worked it out. Now listen. Of all the soldiers over there, there's still less than one percent killed. He'll be all right, Evvie. Lord knows I didn't teach him much, but I did teach him to keep how to keep his head down."

Because of the mess on the table, they eat in the living room. They sit on the sofa, balancing their plates on their laps. Mel studies her face in silence. Without makeup, her dark hair loose and falling to the center of her back, she still looks like a girl. He wonders if her chambray shirt belongs to one of his sons or if a boyfriend left it behind. They have boyfriends, don't they? Even lady preachers?

Evelyn smiles when he takes the plates to the kitchen, running water over them before the egg yolk has a chance to dry. The clutter of the house always bothered him when they were married. Now it feels familiar, comfortable.

"Remember how we used to fight because you left dishes piled up all over the house?"

"It wasn't just dishes. I left cigarettes burning in ashtrays, my clothes wherever they happened to drop. You have to admit, the place was a pigsty."

"Sounds like grounds for divorce to me," he says. But the joke falls flat and she looks away.

They both know that wasn't why he left her. His brother told him more than once, straight out, that everybody in the county knew how Evelyn spent her nights when Mel was on the road. He spent a long time thinking about that, trying to picture her drunk and naked in another man's arms. But it made him feel like somebody trapped at the bottom of a river, the water filling his lungs up, pushing out the air. For months he wouldn't even ask her about it. He dreaded what she might say.

As he watches her scour dried egg from the bottom of the skillet, his arm touching hers, Mel wishes he could ask her why it took her so long to pull herself together, why she had to hurt him so bad to do it, why she had to hurt herself. But before he can even frame the question, the pan disappears under the rinse water and comes up clean.

They spend the day like married people. Evelyn types a paper for her Monday class. Mel changes the oil in his truck. That afternoon, they watch a video of an old Dirty Harry movie. Every time Clint Eastwood narrows his eyes and peers down the barrel of a gun, Evelyn hides her eyes against Mel's sleeve. When they go out for dinner, she tries to pay half, but Mel snatches the ticket away. "Now you're being ridiculous. Who paid for breakfast?"

That evening they play gin rummy and she beats him. It tickles him to watch the pleasure she gets out of winning. She keeps a poker face through each hand, but he figures sooner or later, he's going to catch her with a bundle. She won't lay her spreads down as she gets them, but holds onto each card, picking up his discards with a sly smile.

"Don't gloat, Evelyn," he says, tallying up the final score. He stacks the cards neatly, then tosses them onto the coffee table, where they spew out again. He looks at her left hand, which rests palm down on the arm of the sofa. "Do you ever miss being married?"

She grins. "To you or to Jake?"

18

"Either. No. Me, I guess. Do you ever miss being married to me?"

"Do you miss it?"

"I miss knowing where home is. I miss having somebody to take care of. Wayne never needed taking care of. The army's taking care of Ben. Better than we did."

"Is that why you married me? To take care of me?"

"Why are you asking all the questions? Why do you always do this to me? I asked you first."

"Yes. Sometimes I miss being married. But I don't guess I miss it enough to ever go back to living with somebody again."

"It sure is odd, you making a preacher."

Evelyn lifts her iced tea, and, with her sleeve, wipes away the ring of moisture underneath the glass. "You really think so? You always said I was looking for something, you just didn't know what. Why are you so surprised I found it?"

"Because you used to scare me, some of the places you looked. I never knew how to protect you. I never knew what you wanted me to do."

"I know it." She pushes her hair behind her ear. An earring glitters like a goldfish swimming into the light. "I'm sorry, Mel. I didn't know what I wanted you to do, either."

Mel settles back on the plaid sofa. Evelyn stays on the floor. His knee rests in the space between her shoulder blades. "We used to have a lot of fun," he says. "Remember when we took that old Corvair cross-country and had to hitchhike home?"

She laughs. "I knew it wouldn't make it, but I didn't want to tell you. I was afraid you'd say we couldn't go."

He remembers that trip, nearly a month long. He remembers camping with Evelyn in the Badlands. One night, she woke him up close to dawn to follow a trail they had found the night before and watch the sun come up. Mel remembers following her up terrain that was treacherous even in the daytime, with only their bobbing flashlights to keep them from stumbling and warn the snakes Mel knew with certainty lay coiled in the crumbling leaves at the edge of the dirt trail.

Because it was dark, Mel couldn't see how high up they were, but he could guess from the steep angle of their climb. There was just enough light from the crooked finger of moon and a net of stars to illuminate the jagged landscape of crumbling rock.

Evelyn, of course, wasn't content to go slowly, feeling her way along. She walked so close to the edge that even now, twenty-five years later, Mel can still remember the prickles of anxiety at the back of his neck.

"Why didn't you do things like that after you left me?"

"I don't know. Suddenly you were gone, and you weren't always there, telling me to be careful, and I didn't need to anymore."

Through the open window, he smells the honeysuckles that choke the chained-link fence beside the trailer. Cars on the highway swish by in the light summer rain like girls in satin dresses over crinolines. He remembers Evelyn all dressed up for their senior prom. She looked so small, even with her hair piled high on her head and tottering in her black high heels. She tucked the red carnations he brought her into the hair above her ear, and under her dark lipstick, her teeth looked straight and white.

Mel lifts her hair, seeing her like the double exposure of a slide, the woman sitting in front of him, broad-shouldered and capable, the slight-figured girl pausing in the doorway, already impatient to leave him far behind. He rubs her shoulders and she relaxes against his leg. He leans forward to lightly kiss the back of her neck. Then, with his hand on her chin, he nudges her face around.

She stirs, but instead of turning toward him, she shifts position and moves away. She puts a rubber band around the cards. Then she reaches to the floor for a basket of silk flowers, a Mother's Day gift from Wayne. She places it back in the center of the table carefully, as though she is planting it in concrete, where it can never again be moved.

She starts to say something, falters, and then tries again. "We're just tired, Mel. And feeling lonesome. I'm not even the same person anymore. It'd be like making love to a ghost."

℘ℛ

He sleeps on the couch and gets dressed the next morning while she sleeps. He puts a note on the television, along with some money he knows she needs, but, considering where it came from, won't spend, at least not on herself. By nine he's dropped his load of lumber, and by early afternoon, he's headed southwest out of Louisville with a new load.

On I-24 he picks up a girl who says she's thumbing to New Orleans. She has long blonde hair, and even under layers and layers of makeup, her face looks young. They don't look a thing like each other, but something about the way she tilts her head when she climbs into the truck reminds him of Evelyn.

"Hello, little darling," he says, watching her settle into the seat. Between the hem of her cropped shirt and her low-slung blue jeans, the silver bar in her navel dimples up at him like a second smile. "Aren't you a little young to be hitching rides?"

She shrugs and takes out a cigarette. Without offering Mel one, she drops the package back into her blue canvas bag. When he has pulled back onto the highway, Mel tries again. "I'm serious. Don't you ever watch the news? All kinds of lunatics prowl these highways just looking for sweet young things like you."

She's crawled into the truck as easily as if she's known him all

21

her life. Now she gazes unconcerned across fields that flatten steadily as the land stretches west. She answers him without bothering to turn around. "I'm careful. Won't nobody bother you if you're careful."

Mel studies the brown ridge of bone at the center of her narrow back. Last month he had coffee with a state trooper in a truck stop just west of Cookeville, Tennessee. The trooper said that a few days before, he and his partner found a young girl in a ditch off the interstate, her chest plugged like a watermelon, semen flaked on her thin white thighs.

Mel wants to give this information to the girl as a piece of evidence, to make her understand that some time she might have to pay for taking all these chances, that the world isn't always as safe as it seems.

But her tanned back silences him, and he sighs. "Well, little darling," he says, checking his rearview mirror before he steers into the passing lane. "If New Orleans is a far as you're going, at least this one time, you've got me to take you safe all the way."

Silas Partin and the Pearl of Great Price

When Didi married Silas Partin, Mama tried to tell her he was crazy. But who could have predicted it would take Mama and her Bible to finally push him over the edge?

"Let me get this straight, now," Mama says. "You marry a boy that drinks, smokes dope, and runs around on you. Now he gets saved and wants to be a preacher, and you're mad?"

Didi turns around and looks toward the road, shaking her head. Mama is a fine one to talk, she thinks. Mama herself has been married three times in her thirty-seven years. This doesn't count the string of men who have wandered in and out of Mama's life like vagrants ever since Didi can remember. Men are Mama's weakness, like Aunt Louise's designer purses and Aunt Lindy's taste for sweet pink wine, but there's nothing Mama can tell Didi about Silas that Didi doesn't already know. They've been married eight years, and Didi knew as soon as the honeymoon in Gatlinburg was over that she'd have to go out and make something of herself, if she and Silas were going to have anything.

She went out that very day—her seventeenth birthday—and got a job at a gas station on the outskirts of town. For five years, Didi went to work at 4 a.m., even on Christmas Day, to open up the station and make the sausage biscuits for the truck drivers. Then she studied for her GED and went on to get grants and loans to get into the nursing program at the community college, working at the same time.

It's not that Silas won't work. It's just that he won't stick with anything. Didi has always been the one to think about the future. Sometimes, to tell the truth, she feels more like Silas's mother than his wife. Once, when she told him this, he just laughed and pushed her down on the bed, tracing her ear and throat with his sweet, sweet kisses. "Be good to me, Mama," he said, and oh, she remembered then that there is more to life than the deed to their little house on Maple St. and money in the bank.

When they first got married, Silas hung drywall for a builder. What time he wasn't working, he played the mandolin in bluegrass band. Didi went to all the gigs she could. She loved listening to Silas. He played the mandolin like a percussion instrument, his long, bushy blonde hair flying out around his face as he flung his head back and forth in time to the music. He kept his eyes closed like he wasn't so much playing his mandolin as making love to it.

What bothered Didi was all the drinking and drugs that went along with being in a band. Silas stayed drunk as much as he stayed sober. But even when Didi was mad at him, she never thought about leaving. Then, a year after the band started, as if to reward her for believing in him, he reformed, though it wasn't Didi that brought this change about. One Saturday night, after he had drunk almost a fifth of Jack Daniels, Silas fell off a trampoline at four o'clock in the morning in Joe Whitney's back yard. He fractured his neck and had to wear one of those rubbery collars around it for six months, during which time, he didn't drink so much as a beer.

When the neck brace came off, Silas put his mandolin in the case—he said his heart just wasn't in it anymore—and took a job as a route driver for Frito-Lay. He made good money, but instead of asking Didi if she needed anything for the house, Silas went in debt for a used boat with a cuddy cabin. The boat was longer than their little house. It made Didi mad every time she pulled into the driveway and saw it looming over the little Bradford pear tree she had planted by the back porch.

It made her even madder the times she came home and the boat was gone. Silas went out on the lake on weekends when Didi worked the swing shift, and when he came home the first time smelling like cocoanut sun tan oil and Southern Comfort, she could read the signs.

Didi warned Silas that her friend Brenda's parents had a runabout and a cabin close to the falls where Silas took the boat. "If I take off early from work some night and come down there," she said, "I'd better not catch you even looking at another woman."

Of course, Silas said, "No, honey, you won't." But later Didi didn't know if that meant he wouldn't do anything or she wouldn't catch him, but before she could ask, he bent and kissed her on the nose. Then he went back to winding up the ski rope. He said, "What are you worried about, girl? You know I always come home to you."

But of all the stages Silas has been through, this religious stage is absolutely the worst. For one thing, it's lasted longer than any of the others, nearly two years. After she dated a widowed preacher for a month, one who came through preaching a revival, Mama got religion, and she couldn't rest until Silas and Didi had religion, too. Finally, Silas went to church with Mama one Sunday and got saved while Didi was pulling a double shift at the hospital. Now, only a month after being ordained a minister of God, he's had a falling out with the preacher down at the church over the way the preacher interprets scripture. Silas wants to quit driving the Frito-Lay truck and start his own church.

"You don't understand, Mama," Didi says, brushing a pill bug off the porch step of Mama's trailer. "It's not him preaching I object to. It's just that he wants to be a preacher twenty-four hours a day. He follows me around, reading the Bible to me, like I can't even read it for myself. Like he's been to seminary or something and actually knows what the hell he's talking about. I can't even listen to the Dixie Chicks while I mop the floor or clean the bathrooms, because he takes my CD out and turns on the Christian radio station. It's like living with damn John the Baptist!"

Mama flies up off the porch and looks down at Didi. She points a red polished nail and shakes it at Didi's nose. "Don't you ever say John the Baptist's name and cuss in the same breath. What did they teach you at that college? Sounds to me like Silas is better off figuring out the Lord's word on his own!"

Didi stands up with her car key in her hand. She wants to say, Oh, come off it, Mama. Who are you trying to fool anyway? As soon as some man comes along who'd rather drink than quote scripture, you'll forget all about that white church house down the hill. Instead, she holds her tongue. She knows Mama, she knows Silas, and though she loves them both, Didi learned a long time ago that trying to talk sense into either one of them is like peeing in the wind.

Throughout her shift, Didi feels a sinking spell every time she thinks about Silas. When she pulls into their driveway at 7:30, she sees the light on in the kitchen. Silas is up already, working on his sermon. Bleary-eyed, she leans her forehead on the cold steering wheel, just a little nauseous, dreading to go in. It's December in Kentucky, and though the daytime temperature was in the upper fifties before Didi went to work, a cold front has swept down from Canada during the night, dropping the temperature below freezing. Light snow falls, sticking to the grass. Didi thinks about just backing out of the driveway and leaving. But where would she go? Brenda said a nurse could get a job anywhere, and the two of them ought to just climb in the car and drive all the way to California, get away from here. But Didi is a country girl. She wouldn't even know how to act in California.

Silas looks up when she comes in the kitchen door. He sits at the table, the Bible open in front of him. He doesn't even smile at her anymore, she thinks. He's too busy thinking. But this time, he gets up and pulls out her chair. "Here," he says. "Let me have your coat, honey. I've got some coffee on. You want some?"

She nods and sinks into the chair, resting her elbows on the table. She watches him pour the coffee, uneasy. He never pours her coffee in the morning. He stirs some cream in her coffee and sets it on the table in front of her. "Brother David is off doing a revival in Georgia. I'm preaching today. I thought you might want to go with me for once and hear my sermon."

"Silas," she says. "Honey. I'm wore completely out. I couldn't stay awake for the second coming."

His face darkens. "Now that I'm preaching," he says, "you really ought not to say things like that. People might think you're making light of the Lord."

Didi sighs. When he first started preaching, she tried to go with him on Sunday mornings, but the truth is, even when she's rested, listening to Silas preach makes her nervous. When he played the mandolin, even though he was full of himself, strutting around like he thought any minute some man in a suit was going to come up to the stage and offer him a contract to be a regular Nashville recording artist, at least the music was something she could enjoy and understand.

But this preaching! It's not that she isn't a believer. It's just that all the shouting and hallelujahs make her feel the way she did once when she was twelve and came upon Mama naked. She had gotten up to go to the bathroom, and there was Mama climbing into the shower with a strange man. Mama had her back to Didi, but the man looked across Mama's shoulder and saw Didi and winked and put his hand right on Mama's butt and squeezed it like he wanted Didi to see. Didi slammed the bathroom door hard and went outside to pee behind a bush. Parked outside their trailer was a white Cadillac. The next day the man and Mama took Didi and Billy to Aunt Louise's for the weekend and she didn't come back to get them for a month.

Didi sips the coffee and looks at Silas. God, how she loves him. Some men clean up good, but Silas looks best to her when he's just gotten out of bed, his blonde hair sticking up in every direction. She wants to comb it for him with her fingers, take him to bed, and get him to forget about this craziness.

He sits at the table and turns the Bible so that the print faces her. He slides it a little in her direction. "This is my text," he says. "I got out the Bible this morning and opened it. I just closed my eyes and pointed. This was the very place my finger landed. It's taken from the Book of Luke." He turns the book toward him and reads the passage to her. "Again, the kingdom of heaven is like unto a merchant man, seeking goodly pearls: who, when he had found one pearl of great price, went and sold all that he had, and bought it."

He looks up at Didi expectantly, his blue eyes wide, but she has no earthly idea what he's talking about. "You see, don't you? He says the man sold everything he had, *everything* he owned, to buy that one pearl. Don't you see, Didi? It's a sign."

"A sign of what?"

Silas doesn't answer. He runs his fingers through his hair, his elbows on the table, and his hands clasped at the back of his head as he leans over the Bible. Suddenly, he lifts his head and looks at Didi. "You know that old Winn-Dixie building?" he asks. "The one that's been empty for so long?"

She nods, warily.

"Wouldn't it make a fine church house? Now, I know it would take some fixing up. I'd have to have some seed money. If I had the money out of this house, I could—" Silas stops and looks at her, as if he's expecting her to finish his sentence for him.

Didi rubs her temples. She tries to listen harder to what Silas is saying, but the words are all garbled, like the voice of the teacher in those old Peanuts specials.

"We could put it on the market and have it sold by spring," he says. "And it's not like we wouldn't have a place to live. Your mama said we could move in with her till we got back on our feet."

"Why in the world would I want to move in with Mama? Christ, Silas. How long do you think that would last?"

"But she's different now. She's saved, Didi. And don't say Christ like it's a cuss word. You might as well cut me with a knife."

Didi has never been one to cuss. She has always tried to be quiet and hide herself under big tee shirts and jeans, to show how different she was from Mama with her sassy mouth and tight clothes. But it seems the stronger Mama and Silas have gotten in their religion, the more Didi wants to cuss, cuss, cuss. "Shit," she says. "You're kidding. You want to sell our house? Shit."

Silas stands, leaning over her. "I'm warning you, Didi. You cannot speak that way in my house."

Didi stands up suddenly, knocking the chair over with a thud so loud it scares her. She studies Silas in silence. Then she leans down, picks the chair up, and sets it gently upright. She wants to say, In *your* house. In *your house!* Instead, she picks up the Bible and holds it open. She shoves it under Silas's nose, poking the page so hard with her left index finger that for a moment she's afraid she's torn a hole in the fragile tissue paper. "It says the man bought a pearl, Silas. A pearl! You show me one place in here, one place, where it says to sell your house and lease the old Winn-Dixie."

Silas takes the Bible from her hands and closes it. He lays it gently on the counter, sheltering it from her gaze, as though to keep it safe from her. "I can see there's no use talking to you. If you don't watch out, God's going to show you who's the boss, Didi. I don't know if it'll happen in a wreck, or what, but you mark my words, girl. What happened to that sweet girl I married? You're acting crazy."

In March, Silas gets his own revival to preach, forty-five miles from their house, and Didi doesn't see much of him for two weeks. She thinks maybe he's forgotten about selling the house, until a realtor calls on her day off. Didi tells him, "We're not putting the house on the market. You've been misinformed!" and slams the phone down. But she wonders how long she can hold out against a man who for eight years has been used to getting his way.

At work the next night, the doctor on call makes a pass at her, and she has a chance to take out her frustration on him. He puts his arm around her, looking over her shoulder at her chart. "You're looking sad, Didi," he says. "Why don't you go with me to get some coffee and see if I can cheer you up?"

God, she thinks. He is so good-looking and so slimy, with his shiny, capped teeth and his freshly highlighted, blow-dried hair. In his white coat, he looks like one of the drug lords in the old *Miami Vice*. From what she hears, he's made his way through the nurses under thirty one by one, but the best Didi has to offer him is to fix him up with Mama.

She is so mad she taps the ring finger of the hand that lies damp across her shoulder. "So which one of us wants to invite your wife?"

She leaves her shift early, just after midnight, headed home with a headache, but when she pulls into the driveway, Silas's truck isn't there. Didi rubs her pounding temples. Where the hell is he? It's a nasty night, with rain pelting the windshield. Didi doesn't want to go inside the dark house and lie there alone, worrying. She backs the car out and heads toward Mama's.

Mama's trailer is the last one in the mobile home park, on a cul-de-sac, one of the few trailers that has a built-on porch and a little bit of yard. When Didi sees the blue pick-up parked in front, she pulls behind it, looking at the Jesus Is My Co-Pilot bumper sticker on the tailgate.

The only light on is the one in the kitchen. I guess we all need somebody to tell our troubles to, she thinks, but couldn't Silas find someone else besides Dee's mother? She imagines them at the counter drinking coffee, Silas bent over his Bible and Mama in one of those fluffy nylon robes she wears.

She gets out of the car and goes to the front door. The door is slightly open, and Didi pushes it the rest of the way and goes into the living room. She hears laughter, but it isn't coming from the kitchen. Didi hesitates, feeling dizzy. Surely, not, she thinks. Even Mama wouldn't go this far.

She walks toward the bedroom, past the television with the portrait of Jesus hanging over it, the one that shows Him knocking at the door.

But Didi doesn't need to knock. The bedroom door is open, and apparently Mama and Silas don't hear Didi, because they don't stop what they're doing until she's standing at the foot of the bed. They're wound so tight around each other, it's hard to tell where Mama stops and Silas begins. Mama sees Didi first. She clutches Silas's shoulder and she shakes it hard. When he rolls over, Mama tugs the sheet to cover her breasts. "Oh, baby," she says.

Didi turns around and walks into the living room to wait, though she couldn't say what she's waiting for. She hears Silas and Mama behind her, tugging on their clothes. Mama follows close behind Didi, clutching her powder-blue robe together with her right hand. "Oh, baby," she says again.

Didi sits on the arm of the sofa. "I'm not a baby," she says. "Don't call me baby."

Mama kneels by Didi's feet, looking up at her. Didi turns her head toward the light in the kitchen. "How could you do that, Mama?" she says. "With Silas."

"He's been coming over lately and talking to me. He's upset about you, about how you won't support his ministry. I was just comforting him, like he was one of my babies, like you or Billy. Well, one thing just led to another. We didn't mean to." Mama looks at Didi with a wistful smile, as if she is the child and Didi is the mama, and if she can find the right way to explain it, she can make Didi's anger go away.

But Didi shakes her head. All her life she's been torn between loving Mama and being embarrassed as hell at her. She remembers how Mama used to come to school when Didi was little, wearing a black tank top and jeans so tight Didi expected a ripping noise when Mama sat down at one of the little desks. One year, Didi remembers, Mama had her in three different schools, because every time one of the teachers pissed her off, Mama would show up at school and throw a fit, holding Billy on her hip and dragging Didi out by the arm. Didi would be mortified, but also triumphant. She couldn't take up for herself, but Mama could. Mama, as she herself would tell anybody within earshot, didn't take shit from nobody.

"Of course you didn't mean to. You never mean to. What does that even mean? And what am I supposed to do now?" Didi looks at Mama as if Mama might really have an answer. As if she weren't the woman Didi just caught in the bedroom screwing Didi's husband.

And Mama answers the question the same way. "You should have left him a long time ago," Mama says. "Maybe I did you a favor, really, showing you Silas for what he is. He means well. He's just— Well, you're the one married to him. You know what he is."

Didi looks toward the bedroom. The bathroom light is on, but

Silas still hasn't come out to face her. Coward. Didi stands up and starts toward the bedroom, but instead she stops and looks down at Mama's face, streaked with tears and mascara. She has never been so angry in her life. "Jesus," she says. "You did me a favor? Jesus. What were you thinking?"

But Mama wasn't thinking. Thinking is not Mama's strong point.

Didi stands up and shakes her head again, as if she's got cobwebs in her brain and can't get them cleared. She jumps when a gust of wind bangs the door hard, and then shivers and looks to see what made the noise. She must have left the door open when she came, but she doesn't know when she walks over if she plans to shut it and turn back to confront Silas or to go out it and never come back. But once she touches the knob, she walks on through, slams the door behind her, and runs to the car through the rain.

At her house, she starts packing, and she's calm as ice. Good luck to them if they think they'll be hearing from her any time soon. Thank God for the pill. Thank God she had sense enough to use it. Because there are no children, she has no ties to Silas, no reason even to talk to him for a long, long time. There's quite a bit of equity in the house, but she doesn't think he can sell it without her signature. She remembers seeing in a movie once that it takes seven years after a person disappears to declare her legally dead. Let him twist for a while, she thinks. Let him twist forever.

It's almost daylight when she has the possessions she's taking packed into her car. Above the tree line the fading moon glimmers in the sky like the inside of a broken oyster shell. She doesn't have a plan, but she has a nursing degree and an atlas and west looks like a good direction. For the first time since Silas started hounding her about being born again, she thinks she knows what he means.

Fault Lines

When Carlos Helton rounds the corner of his house Wednesday morning, he finds his brother Billy's Taurus parked in the driveway. Through the screen door, he hears his wife Sue singing, but not straight through and effortlessly, the way she sings when she works. Between phrases, Billy stops to give her instructions, giving her the pitch on the piano one note at a time.

On the top step, Carlos bends to take off his boots. Letting the screen door shut softly behind him, he sets them on the newspapers Sue has laid out for him, the only thing out of place in the spotless room. The old upright piano stands catty-corner at the far end of the long kitchen. Billy sits on a ladder back chair in front of the piano. He has a gold sweater draped around his shoulders with the sleeves tied in the front. Sue leans across him, looking at the music. Her hand rests on the chair back, her forearm just touching his shoulder.

"That sure is some pretty music," Carlos says, and they both turn around.

Sue lets go of the chair suddenly and slides both hands into the pockets of her jeans. The eye shadow she has on makes her eyes look green. Carlos tries to remember. Did she put on make-up early this morning, or did she wait until she saw Billy's car at the bottom of the hill? And why does it matter? After all, Billy is his brother.

"You scared me to death," she says, pushing a dark strand of hair behind her ear. She smiles, blushing, looking up at Carlos. "Does it really sound good? Billy wants me to sing this song Sunday by myself. My first solo."

Billy stands, too. The hand he holds toward Carlos is long-fingered, the nails shiny and even. "How's it going, buddy? I see you're up with the chickens."

Carlos raises his own hands into the air to show how sticky they are from the tobacco. Then he backs to the sink. Sue keeps dishwashing liquid on top next to the faucet, and Carlos squirts some into the palms of his hands. He doesn't like his brother being here much, and it makes him feel awful to admit this, even to himself. Billy is between jobs and has come home for a year while he finishes up his master's thesis. With Daddy in Lone Oak Assisted Living, this seemed a good time to come home. At least, that's Billy's story. Carlos thinks there's more to it than Billy's letting on.

When Carlos finishes at the sink, Billy has sat down again, his long fingers splayed to make a chord at the piano. He sings the notes in falsetto, to show Sue where she went wrong. Carlos pours himself a cup of coffee and listens to them. The cup clatters when he sets it in the sink, hard, but neither of them turns around.

"Guess I'd better get on back to work," he says. "Sue, I need you down there, too, as soon as you can get away." He pauses at the doorway, but Sue keeps looking at the sheet music. In farewell, Billy turns his head sideways toward Carlos and wiggles it up and down, chording with his left hand, while he traces the pattern of notes for Sue with his right.

Their boys are working down the hill in the barn. The old building is dim and dusty, even with the big front doors propped open to let in some light. Near the stripping tables, Andrew, the youngest boy, draws back a tobacco stick, aiming it at his brother like a spear. Carlos reaches over the boy's shoulder and takes the stick from him. "Quit," he says, though talking to Andrew is like talking to a rock. Even when he was a baby, he could scream in his crib for hours. The books Sue read said that if parents left a baby to cry it out, the baby would last maybe thirty minutes. Well, the experts didn't know Andrew. Now, sixteen and six foot three, he still wants to be up all night, raising who knows what kind of hell and getting into who knows what kind of trouble.

Sue is always after Carlos to talk to Andrew, but what would he say? The truth is, Carlos was a lot like Andrew when he was young. When he wasn't working on the farm or at football practice, he spent every spare minute running with some of the other football players, drinking beer and fishing down at the river. They'd listen to the old stuff on somebody's tape player—Jimi Hendrix and Charlie Daniels and Lynard Skynard—and talk about getting laid. Talking was all most of them knew how to do. Carlos hopes that Andrew is all swagger and talk, too, and that, sooner or later, Andrew will just grow out of it, the way Carlos did, when a two-hundred and fifty-pound linebacker put an end to Carlos's football scholarship and Daddy's dreams, and Carlos finally had to grow up and figure out how to make a living.

Jon looks up gratefully at Carlos. Then, with fingers almost as nimble and quick as his father's, he bends over the table to tie a handful of leaves together at the top and bottom with strips of tobacco. From the house, they hear Billy playing the piano and Sue singing.

Carlos takes an armload of tobacco and flings it into the truck bed hard enough to send dust swirling into the air. He is always hard to live with during tobacco season. It's even worse this year with a depressed market, a note due at the bank at the end of

December, and Billy making Sue dissatisfied, just when Carlos thought she had finally settled in.

But Carlos loves this place, and no matter how hard it is to make a living here, he can't imagine being anywhere else. It's not as if he hasn't tried. After he and Sue got married, he left the farm to take a job as an assistant manager in a department store chain. The store had transferred him to three different cities in six years when his father called to tell Carlos his mother was dying. Probably, the doctor said, from breathing his father's cigarette smoke for so many years. But his daddy maintained right up to the funeral that the doctor was full of horse manure. "Think about it," he said, in the car on the way to the cemetery. "It don't make no sense, does it? I'm the one been smoking. If it was tobacco give a body cancer, don't it seem like they'd be burying me?"

When they do bury his daddy, will there be anybody left who understands the way Carlos feels about this place, or about anything else? He tries and tries to explain to Sue, but it just wears them both out, even though Sue is always wanting to talk about their problems (she calls it "their relationship"). Carlos thinks talking is over-rated. Some things you just have to know in your bones.

Daddy was against Sue from the beginning, but Carlos believed that when Daddy really got to know her, he would love her just as Carlos did. Not that Carlos himself understood why he loved her. She wouldn't give Carlos the time of day in high school, but the more he pursued her, and the more she said no, the more he wanted her. He took another girl to the senior prom, a prettier girl, to tell the truth, but he spent the whole night looking over the girl's shoulder, trying to catch glimpses of Sue looking awkward and too tall in a blue satin dress. A few strands of her dark hair had slipped free from its carefully sprayed up-do and curled around the edge of her shoulders when she danced.

Then, her sophomore year at college, Sue came home at Christmas and gave him a call. "You still want to date me?" she said. He could have sworn she was crying.

"I do," he said.

"You know where I live?"

"In town? In that white house on the corner of Elm St. and Blair?"

"That's the one. Pick me up at seven."

Sue didn't go back to school in January, and by March, they were married. This was entirely Sue's idea. Carlos would never have dared to ask her. Loving her was like waiting silent and still in a deer blind. He had wanted her so long, and now she had come home and offered herself to him. After all his patience, why take the chance of making the one wrong move that might chase her away?

Daddy was breaking up dirt in a sheltered spot to plant winter lettuce when Carlos went out to tell him he had a new daughter-in-law. Daddy kept digging the whole time Carlos was talking. When Carlos finished, Daddy stopped and leaned on the handle of the shovel. "I'm telling you," he said, shaking his head. "She won't like it out here." For the first time, Carlos wondered if he had made a terrible mistake.

Daddy was right, and when Sue wanted Carlos to leave and take a job in the city, he left. She mesmerized him, that's what she did, but there was something about her, about the way he could never be sure of her, that made him like it. Besides, by the time he knew—at least in his heart—that he would never be able to keep her, they had Jon to think of. Then it didn't seem either of them had a choice, and he could relax his hold on her, his way of watching her, always at the edge of his consciousness, the way farmers keep checking the air for signs of rain.

On the way back to Knoxville after his mother's funeral,

Carlos said, in a low voice to keep from waking up the boys, who were asleep in the back seat, "The farm's going to be a handful with just Daddy left. He's not getting any younger. I know he could use some help."

"He can hire help."

"Hired help will steal you blind, you don't have somebody looking out for you."

Sue studied her hands, turning her wedding ring around and around on her finger. The knuckle above it had thickened until she needed soapy water to get the ring off. "It's a wonder he's lasted this long. Not much of a life, is it, living hand to mouth and every year going more in debt than out? I don't think I could stand it, Carlos. I couldn't stand it for a day."

The next morning, without talking to her first, Carlos gave the store notice and called from a pay phone, asking Daddy to get the old rental house cleaned up. Carlos was bringing his family home.

ॐ

It's warm in the barn this time of day, even in late November, and Carlos swipes his hand impatiently across his forehead, smearing the dirt and sweat. It's not as though he hasn't tried to be good to her. Reaching for another bundle of hands Andrew has tied, Carlos says, "Jon, run up to the house and get your mother. We could use a little help down here."

When Sue comes to the barn twenty minutes or so later, she glares at Carlos. "I was coming," she says, low, when her work brings her close enough for him to hear. "You didn't need to send Jon after me."

"Hey, don't start in on me," Carlos says. He spits tobacco juice on the dry dirt beside the truck tire and watches it gather like a glob of mercury from a broken thermometer. "I didn't say a damned thing. But tell me this. If Billy is so goddamned smart, what's he wasting a year of his life here for? This ain't exactly no music capital of the world."

In January, Billy lands a job with a high school one county over, replacing a chorus teacher on pregnancy leave. His fiancé moves down from Louisville to live with him, and that, Carlos figures, will at least do him in with the Baptists at the little church they attend, where Billy directs the choir. But it seems Billy can follow his own rules. Even Daddy makes over Billy. At church, when Billy parks his new car next to Carlos's beat-up old pickup, Daddy tells everybody he can get to stand still long enough to listen how Billy went off to college and made something of himself.

But who stayed? Carlos wants to ask Daddy. Who got up early and picked you up and brought you to church? Doesn't that count for something, too? But he doesn't say anything. What good would it do?

When Lisa has been there a few days, Sue invites the two of them for supper. Lisa is short, pear-shaped, and skinny, except for the span of her hips. At supper, she scoots up close to the oak table and leans forward to slide a wedge of glazed ham from the platter onto her plate. "I just love good country cooking," she says.

"I'm glad to see her eating," Billy says. He smiles at her, the caps on his teeth as white as the rims on their mother's good china. "She doesn't eat enough to keep a bird alive. I'm glad she's moved down here for good so I can take care of her."

For good? Carlos thinks.

Lisa blushes and reaches a tiny, red-tipped finger over to press his hand. "Oh, you are so sweet. Don't you think he is so sweet?"

Carlos smears butter on an ear of corn. He can think of other words for Billy, but he keeps them to himself. This must be what

Sue means when she says Carlos doesn't know how to show his feelings. Well, she might be glad of that tonight, if she could guess even half the feelings he's been holding in.

"Sue," Carlos says, between bites. "Now Sue here. She can eat me under the table." Sue narrows her eyes at him over a forkful of slaw, and he realizes at once he's stumbled. He knows she worries about her weight, though she doesn't need to. He heard her tell her friend Brenda at church Sunday it didn't do her any good to go on a diet. For every twenty pounds she lost, she found twenty-five. How could he forget that? Why can't she realize he's just teasing her?

"I don't mean anything bad by it," he says, trying to repair the damage, but digging himself in deeper with every word. This is one night he just can't seem to shut up. "Sue's a strong woman. She can lift as much as Andrew can. Me, I don't have any use for a woman who won't eat."

Lisa smiles at Sue and pats her on the arm. When she speaks, her voice is condescending, not about Sue's weight, but about Sue's stupid husband. "She has to feed her voice. Billy says she is just the most amazing singer. It takes strength to sing."

After supper, Carlos finds a deck of cards in a drawer in the kitchen. He flips through them to pull out the jokers. "You all play spades?"

Sue's frown—the one she's worn all evening, from the first moment Carlos opened his mouth—deepens. "Not everybody wants to sit around and play cards all night. They might just want to talk. Or Billy might play the piano and we could sing?"

But Billy looks up at Carlos and taps the table once with his index finger. "Deal 'em. But remember how I used to beat you two out of every three."

Carlos gets Lisa for a partner, and she turns out to be a pretty good player. She puts on big round glasses to read the cards, and she keeps up with every trump that's played. He and Lisa win the first two games, and Carlos looks over at Billy. "Now who used to beat who two out of three?'

Before the third game, Sue gets up to slice the chocolate cake. She carries the slices to the table on clear pink dessert plates, Depression glass, he thinks she calls it, and he can't get over how pretty she looks tonight. Her dark hair falls softly over the collar of her red blouse, and her dangly silver earrings glitter in the bright kitchen light. Compared to Lisa, she looks so womanly, with a woman's breasts, not those flat little things that look like fried eggs, or that short raggedy hair that looks like a girl's head got caught in a hay baler. She tilts her head toward Carlos. He wants to say something, but he's just like a boy with a weight on his tongue, and he looks down at the table.

Billy tilts his chair back, his hands laced behind his head. "I've been meaning to talk to you, Carlos. There's a developer in town looking to buy up some property out this way to build a new subdivision. Says this farm could bring top dollar for housing lots. Or we could develop it ourselves, subcontract the building. All you'd have to invest would be the money for water lines and roads, and the houses we'd sell would pay for that and still give us a nice profit."

"It's a farm," Carlos says. "Hard to farm on pavement."

"But that's just it. Why does it have to be a farm? It's land. Just because it's been farmed all these years doesn't mean you have to keep farming it. You can use it for whatever you want to. Besides, Carlos, how long do you think you can hang on out here? Tobacco's your biggest cash crop, right? I mean, come on. Tobacco's been on its way out for thirty years. What are you going to do for labor when the boys go off? Do you really think this place produces enough income for three families to live on? And what about when all the Mexicans start working in that new chicken-processing plant and you can't even pay them to help?"

He waits just the way he used to when he had the winning poker hand and he wanted to see the look on his brother's face when Carlos—even stubborn Carlos—knew it.

But stubborn Carlos isn't ready to give in. "We'll figure something else out. Anyway, it's no concern of yours, Billy. I'm the one working the farm. You let me worry about it."

Billy hardly misses a beat before he lays out his final argument. "But when something happens to Dad—you know the way his health's been, Carlos, and nobody lives forever—it *would* be a concern to me. I wouldn't *make* you buy out my half, but I'd sure try and get you to think about it, and at some point I might have to. Could you do that without selling? It seems like a no-brainer to me. You can work yourself to death like Dad, or you can get out and make some good money, too."

"That's what I've been trying to tell him," Sue says, looking carefully at Billy and avoiding Carlos's eyes. "He loves this place, I know he does, and it would be so hard— But there's no future here."

"Did you know this whole county is on the New Madrid fault line?" Billy asks her. "When the last big earthquake hit, in the eighteen hundreds, it made the Mississippi River run backwards. You'd never know it, would you, just by looking, how unstable the ground is underneath? Let me tell you, nothing lasts forever, not even land."

Carlos picks up the cards dealt for him and fans them out in his hands. He tries not to think about fault lines and bulldozers, about Sue in her red blouse, or the way she looks at Billy as though he hung the moon. He divides the cards up first by color and then by suits. He studies the cards and his heart sinks. Not much to bet on here, now that Billy has finally shown his hand.

He wants to tell Billy that Daddy won't leave Billy half the farm, that he'll talk to Daddy, get him to make out a will so that the land passes to Carlos, who will keep it for his sons and Billy's, who haven't been born yet. But while Carlos has been working the dirt on the farm, what has Billy been working, especially considering the condition of their father's weak, old heart?

When Billy and Lisa leave, Carlos puts on his coat and goes to the barn to check on the animals, his flashlight bobbing circles in front of him in the dark. He keeps the milk cows in the barn at night, and he pats the flank of each one as he passes.

At the house, Sue has already gone to bed. He undresses and scoots in beside her. He puts his arm into the curve of her waist. She moves away, and he could pretend to miss her signal, but for some reason tonight, he doesn't want to roll over and let it go. "What did I do?" he says, stubbornly, his hand shaking her by the hip. "Just what in the hell did I do?"

She pulls away from him then and turns her pillow to its cold side, punching it into a wad before she lies back down. "Nothing. You didn't do anything. You never do."

Carlos rolls over on his back and looks up at the ceiling, white and ghostly from the porch light. "Did you know Billy in high school?" he asks. "He went around in that silly white band suit, waving that baton. One son of a bitch was dumb enough to ask me *to my fac*e if I knew my brother was a queer. I'll bet you didn't know that, did you? That everybody thought Billy was a queer?"

Sue sighs, but she doesn't sound angry, just tired. "I hate it when you talk like that. I don't know what you think it proves. Besides, what does Billy have to do with anything?"

He sits up in bed and puts his feet on the cold floor. "You tell me."

"You know you're making a fool of yourself? God, Carlos. Billy's your brother. And anyway, he's crazy about Lisa. They act like two teenagers." She waits a moment or two before she speaks again, and when she does, her voice sounds light, as though she is pleased in spite of herself. "What in the world would Billy want with me?"

Carlos gets up and slips his pants on. Even in the dark, he can feel her smiling. He doesn't know if she is smiling because she sees how Billy looks at her, no matter what kind of show he thinks he's putting on, or if she is laughing at Carlos and his jealousy. But God help him, if he doesn't get out of here fast, he'll knock the smile right off her face.

He wakes up the next morning in his recliner, freezing. He tiptoes into the bedroom in the dark to shut off the alarm before it goes off and wakes Sue. His work shirt from the day before hangs on the post at the foot of the bed. He slips it on and is out of the house before she even knows he is gone.

He drives out to the creek to repair some fences. He doesn't finish until it's nearly dark, but instead of turning up the long driveway toward the lighted windows of his house, he stays on the blacktop and drives. He drives every back road in the county, but they don't seem as much like back roads anymore. How did he miss it when acres of houses with paved, winding streets took over so much of the good farmland? He feels as if as if he went to sleep in one place, where the land stretched green for miles around him, folded here and there into hills, and he woke up to find himself lost in a country full of strangers, where all the landmarks have disappeared.

He shakes his head at his own stubbornness and stupidity. Billy's right. What kind of crazy dream has Carlos been living in? The boys work the farm because they have to, but Andrew will be gone as soon as he's old enough to go. Jon keeps his head buried in a chemistry book and says he wants to be a pharmacist, to spend his whole working life in a space about the size of a horse's stall. Why would they want Carlos to fight Billy to keep the farm in one piece? If he asks them, they will tell him to sell off the land and put the money in their hands.

He doesn't head home until close to ten. Billy's Taurus glimmers in the moonlight near the house. Carlos pulls the pick-up truck next to Billy's car. He opens the door and stands for a moment, watching Sue through the kitchen window, Billy behind her. She looks like she's been crying, and for a moment Carlos's heart races. She's right. He is a fool. She's worried about him. He should have called her. But what would he have said? Billy puts both hands on her shoulders, the way he has more than once before, even while Carlos has been in the room with them, kneading the tension out of her neck, then working his hands from her neck to the tops of her arms and back again. Then, suddenly, he wraps his arms around her waist and pulls her close to him, leaning his cheek against the top of her dark hair.

She stops him. Later, Carlos will remember that she stops him. She takes his hands, unclasps his arms, and moves away. But he will also remember what he can see from the window, though from behind her Billy doesn't—the misery and longing on her face.

He doesn't start the truck when he climbs back into it. He leaves the headlights turned off, puts the truck into neutral, and coasts to the bottom of the hill before he cranks up the engine. He drives a short distance and turns up the road to the other side of the farm, to Daddy's house. The road here is rough, and the truck bounces along. The old moon bounces along, too, low in the sky above him, like a balloon on a string.

At the end of the road, Carlos sits in the truck and studies the old house. When Daddy built it, in the late sixties, it was a house he was proud of, with five good rooms to raise his sons in. Now, Carlos knows, most mobile homes have more square footage and at least two baths. He tries to imagine this house sitting in the middle of a new subdivision where it's against the deed restrictions to hang clothes on a line or park a pick-up truck on the street.

He sits a little longer in the dark, but he has already made up his mind. Then, the plan and action forming together, he takes a five-gallon container from the back of the pickup and splashes gasoline on the weatherboard siding, working his way around the perimeter of the house. He takes firewood from the shed and heaps it on the front porch. Then he pours gasoline on the pile of wood, too.

When the first container is empty, he goes to the truck for another. He carries it inside the front door, into the living room, and sets it down. He takes the family photos off the mantel and carries them out to the truck. Then he gets the photo albums off the bookcase and the bills and papers from Daddy's roll top desk.

When he returns to the house for the third time, he stops and tries to think what else he should carry with him. His football trophies that Daddy still displays in a glass case he had specially made? What about his mother's furniture, darkened by dust and age? But he decides to leave it all behind. No point in carting out junk he'll just have to get rid of later. Billy and Sue have been giving him the same message over and over. He may be slow, but he finally gets it. There is nothing worth saving here.

When he has stacked the photographs and Daddy's papers neatly in the passenger seat of the truck, he goes inside the final time. In the living room, he pours out the gasoline from the second container, walking in circles around the braided rug. When the can is empty, he leaves it in the center of the circle and goes out again. This time he slams the door hard behind him. At the bottom of the porch steps, he kneels in the dirt, takes out the small flashlight he carries in his pocket, and searches the ground. When he finds a stick dry enough, he holds his lighter to the end until it catches fire. Then he tosses the lighted stick onto the porch, and in a few seconds, the wood there catches, too.

He backs the truck a safe distance from the house, and gets out. He is dead tired, but he stays to watch the fire, wondering, as if he's back in high school trying to solve an algebra problem, how long it will take the house to burn down. He knows it will take a fraction of the time it took to build it.

But it burns even faster than that. The place is past saving long before the trucks from the volunteer fire department arrive. He starts walking toward the fire, but a fireman takes him roughly by the shoulder and pulls him back. They don't even bother to get out their gear.

Carlos sits on the ground, and then looks up, surprised to see them. When he wipes the smoke from his eyes, he realizes that he has been crying. The tears drip off his chin like sweat.

Poison

Tiffany stands in the kitchen, looking out the window over the sink. She throws her head back and takes a long drag. This is the best damned pot she's ever smoked, and it makes everything stand out—each leaf of the scrubby Kentucky coffee tree beside the steps, the lights of the police car pulled up next to the front of the neighbor's four doors down. Sometimes she could swear that every weekend she's living in an episode of *Cops*, they have to come around here so often to break up fights or check on break-ins. Mostly the cops leave with their back seats empty, because when it comes down to it, none of the women who call them want to see their boyfriends or ex-husbands go to jail. Like Tiffany's mom, they just want peace for a minute is all, just somebody to come and lay the law down.

The bright blue lights give her a little rush every time they flash on and off, and if she closes her eyes, she can still see the flash against her eyelids. She feels like she's on a ride at one of the endless county fairs that made up her world when her mother was carny trash and not the respectable woman she has tried to become, going to the community college to get a two-year degree in accounting, before she got sick and had to quit.

Mom was pretty when she was young, in a pitiful kind of way, with shiny hair and a scrubbed face, fake turquoise jewelry dangling from her small pink ears. Terry says Mom looks just like a witch, with her thin hair and pointed nose, her eyes as dull as peach pits, no sparkle left in them at all. Tiffany laughs when he says this, even though she knows she shouldn't let him make fun of her mother.

When she traveled with the carnival, Mom wore long, bright-colored skirts and gauzy blouses and talked with a gypsy accent, making her *w*'s sound like *v*'s. To keep up with Tiffany, Mom kept a rope tied around her waist and tied the other end around Tiffany's. Sometimes, with Mom saying day in and day out how much she depends on her baby, it feels like she still does.

Sometimes Tiffany daydreams about moving away with Terry, climbing into the Mustang and driving all the way to the ocean, which she's never even seen. They'll live on the beach, and he'll sit out by the water while she fixes hamburgers on the back porch on a little grill, and she'll show them all, Cletus and those snotty girls at school who draw in their elbows when they walk past her in the hall, afraid of catching whatever they think she has.

When the cop car leaves, she washes what's left of the joint—not much, it was so small it was burning her fingers—down the sink and goes out on the little stoop at the back of the trailer. She sits on the steps and sips beer from a plastic cup. Her skin tingles as she watches the police car bounce up and down over a pothole in the gravel road; it thrills her to think she's been breaking the law not a hundred yards from where they were investigating.

From the body shop across the highway from the trailer park, she can hear the clanging sound of tools against metal and men's voices, laughing. She closes her eyes and imagines Terry leaning in the garage entrance, where she first met him. He's probably wearing his black Johnny Cash tee shirt—the one with Johnny at Folsom Prison, giving the guards the finger—and his jeans tight and ripped out in the knees. He'll be drinking a beer, too, from the can, he always is, supervising the boys who work for his daddy. He doesn't have to work. He's one of those people who have money to burn.

Her heart revs up, like the 440 under the hood of his black Mustang, just thinking about how it felt the other day when Terry kissed her. In a little while, she'll walk over to the Shell station and buy a Coke from the machine, to remind him she's waiting for him.

She takes another sip of her beer and watches a spider spin out a long filament of silk that stretches from the blood red branches of the prickly barberry bush to the rusted wrought iron railing of the tiny stoop. Mom would kill her if she saw her drinking a beer, don't even mention the joint, which of course Mom can't smell because she can't smell anything anymore. Anyway, she doesn't really care what Mom thinks, it's just the aggravation. Cletus doesn't care at all. He tells her, just pour it in a plastic cup and drink while your mom's sleeping and wink, wink, what she don't know won't hurt you, ain't he a good step daddy to treat her so grown-up and keep her secrets for her?

Cletus would like to have a few more secrets between them, but Tiffany can handle an old fart like Cletus. When Mom first met him, he was good-looking in a leathery, cowboy kind of way, but now he's just a soft, red-faced fart with runny pink rabbit eyes resting on her tits or her belly button with its little gold ring. He can look all he wants to, and sometimes he gets a little grab in before she gets away from him, but as long as he antes up with a little pocket money and shares his beer, she'll let him have his little thrill. All he's gonna get, anyway. Let him dream.

It's Cletus's fault they're living in this dump. Mom says if he hadn't accused her of being a drug addict and a hypochondriac after she got poisoned, they could have sued the pesticide company and be living on easy street. Instead, he had to sit in the hospital waiting room and run his mouth, and they lost everything. Because of Mom's reaction to even the mildest chemicals, they had to throw away everything they owned and start over without much money. Even Mom's baby pictures of Tiffany had to go, even the clothes on their backs. Mom had to quit school and can't even clean houses anymore. She can't be around any kind of chemicals. Even the chemicals from photographs or the ink from magazines make her throat and chest tighten until she can't breathe and her arms and legs get completely numb, starting with the tips of her fingers. If she had gotten a settlement, they might have moved out west somewhere, maybe Arizona, without all this Kentucky ragweed just making her sicker by the day.

When the Daniel Boone Forest caught fire last summer, even though the fires were nearly a hundred miles away, the smoke was so toxic to Mom that she made Cletus put duct tape around all the trailer windows. At night, with the lights at the Shell station making the silver tape shine, their trailer looks like something out of *Lost in Space*. When Mom does go outside, which isn't very often, she wears a gas mask she ordered off the Internet to protect herself from the poisons in the air. It's like the ones she saw in an ad in one of Cletus's magazines, as part of a kit to have on hand in case of a chemical attack.

She just about died last weekend when Mom showed up down the road at Misty's wearing it. Mom had on a pilled lime green tank top and some flowered pants that were too short, and add that crazy mask, and she looked like she'd escaped from the mental ward. Tiffany was just cuddled up with Terry on the couch—not even in the bedroom like Misty and her boyfriend—but Mom was so mad, she grabbed Tiffany by the arm and pulled her out the door. She was surprisingly strong for somebody who is not only tiny, but practically an invalid, but Tiffany has seen on *Survivor* how often anger or fear can give people strength above their normal limitations.

She goes back in house to make one more check on things before Terry comes. She tiptoes down the hall and leans her ear against the thin door to see if she can hear her mother snoring. She feels a little bit guilty, but yesterday, when Terry asked her to go out with him tonight she had known Mom would never let her go. Then she had the brilliant idea of how to make sure Mom couldn't stop her.

Because of her condition, Mom will only eat raw foods that she processes in a special juicer she bought from the Home Shopping Club. Tiffany makes Mom a juice cocktail every afternoon, but today she ground up three of Cletus's Percocets (he supposedly has a bad back, and he gets all kinds of stuff prescribed from five or six different doctors and sells what he doesn't use) and put the drug in the juice. Then, to make sure, she emptied a capsule of Benadryl and added two of those little pills— Phenergan?—Mom keeps for her stomach.

Tiffany has had this little nagging feeling all day that there might be a chemical in one the pills that Mom's allergic to. She doesn't want to kill her for goodness sakes, she just wants to have a date. She opens the bedroom door and peeks in; Mom is sprawled out on the bright bedspread, still as a corpse, and Tiffany panics, but when she creeps closer to the bed, she can see Mom's thin chest moving up and down, ever so slightly, her mouth open and her head tipped back on the pillow. Mom has gotten so thin, her elbows stick out like a grasshopper's legs, and her skin is dry as its husk.

Tiffany shuts the door and goes into the kitchen to get another beer. She chugalugs this one because she's so nervous about going out with Terry, nervous and excited all at the same time.

In the bathroom, she checks her makeup in the mirror and flips her short blonde hair up at the back with her hands to make it look messy. She read in a magazine that messy hair makes a girl look sexy, like she just climbed out of bed. The last thing she does is brush her teeth and swish mouthwash around. She doesn't gargle. No point in pushing her luck, gargling would make so much noise.

When she's sure she looks all right, she walks over to the garage. She sees Terry before he sees her, and she stands there, posing, one hand on her hip, waiting for him to turn around. Buddy, the baldheaded man that runs the shop, looks around the car hood of a green pickup and sees her first. He gives a low whistle, and her face turns red—God, these old men are such perverts!—so when Terry looks over and sees her, she doesn't look sexy or sophisticated, she just looks stupid.

He has his cap turned around backwards, and he tips his hand to his forehead in a little salute, God it is so cute how he does that.

"Hey," he says. Then he slithers toward her from where he leans against the garage wall and comes over to where she's standing. "I wondered if you were coming. You want a beer?"

Buddy looks at them over at them, shaking his head, laughing. "We can't be giving beer to minors," he says. "What is she, thirteen?"

Tiffany puts her hand on her hip and fires back at him, the same way she does with Cletus. "I'm eighteen, Buddy Martin. Turned eighteen last Tuesday, I'll have you know." But she's lying through her teeth, and they both know it, and it doesn't make any difference, Terry doesn't care how old she is, and anyway eighteen is still not twenty-one.

The truth is, she's just barely turned sixteen and she was only allowed to get her learners' permit because Cletus is gone so much, and Mom's too sick to drive Tiffany to school or to work afterward at the Dairy Queen. As far as she can tell, that's the only good thing to happen to her since the pesticide company sprayed their apartment and ruined their lives. If Mom didn't have those sick headaches that attack out of nowhere and make her blind as one of Cletus's two-day drunks, there's no way she would have let her even learn to drive.

Terry slides his arm across her shoulders and pulls her close to his side. She has on a powder blue tank top that matches her eyes, and she knows when Terry runs his hand along her bare, tanned arm that she has picked the right clothes. Tiffany lets herself settle against him, tilting her chin up so she can see his face. He smells like aftershave, beer, and gasoline.

He winks at her, then looks toward Buddy. He gives her arm a squeeze, and winks at Buddy and the other guys, too, managing to include her in the conversation and leave her out at the same time. "I don't know, boys. She feels eighteen to me."

He lets go, and from the cooler in the back seat of his Mustang, he gets a beer and hands it to her, popping the flip top with one hand. Then he opens the passenger side for her to slide in.

She has a little flash of apprehension, but what is she afraid of? She won't get caught. The stomach medicine by itself ought to keep Mom asleep for hours. She's a teenager, not a nurse in a rest home. Doesn't she deserve to have some fun once and awhile? She climbs into the car. When Terry gets in on the other side and turns the key, the engine has a sweet low roar, and the stereo's bass boom vibrates all the way down to her spine.

At the lake, Terry kisses her, and they make out for a while. She wants to feel hot and lost the way she did earlier today when she imagined being here, but Terry keeps hurrying her, taking her hand and putting it on his lap, and his hands are rough, poking into her and squeezing her nipples too hard. She wants him to look at her the way boys look at girls in the movies, but she can't get him to slow down. All the way down here, he's been drinking from a fifth of bourbon and smoking a tiny glass pipe that she has to keep lighting for him, watching him beat time on the steering wheel to the punked-up music pouring out of his stereo. Her buzz is wearing off, but he's still flying. He hasn't looked her in the eye once since they left the garage to come out here.

Over the slosh of the creek, she hears the katydids—katydid, katy-didn't, wish katy'd make up her mind. Tiffany had stayed out in the country with her grandparents one summer when her mom was in rehab because of meth and oxy. She'd sit with Grandpa on the front porch of their little yellow house. He'd say that same phrase every night, as if he'd just thought it up. She was thirteen, and she thought he was stupid, but she always laughed in spite of herself.

All three of them got teary-eyed when her mother came back to get her, but as Tiffany waved to them from the window of Mom's car, she couldn't help thinking they were glad to see her go.

Terry is pushing her head down, and she thinks she says, wait, but even she isn't sure she said anything, so of course he doesn't. It doesn't matter anyway because his cell phone rings, a rap phrase he downloaded from the Internet that makes her ears hurt, and he pushes her away to answer it. She chugs some of the bourbon and leans back in the seat, looking out at the path of moonlight trembling on the top of the creek water. The liquor burns, but she doesn't want to be left behind Terry, and she takes another drink, holding her nose so she can't taste the bourbon, and drinking as much as she can straight down.

Cradling the phone between his ear and shoulder, Terry pats her arm, motioning toward the bag of dope on the dashboard. She takes another long drink from the bottle. Then she opens the baggie and puts some into the bowl of the pipe, handing it to Terry.

He takes the pipe in his right hand and packs the dope down with his thumb. He's nodding and the other person is talking as he puts the stem between his teeth and lights the pipe. He takes a hit and then hands it off to her.

She sucks the stem hard, the bowl glowing, and then hands it back to Terry. After two or three hits, alternated with the bourbon, she's flying again, too, just as Terry is sobering up a little. He sits up straight behind the steering wheel and gestures as he talks, something about, how long is he going to be here? and oh, man, we used to really party, and, I've got a little something to take care of here first, but tell him I'll be there as soon as I can.

And suddenly, she's flying out across the creek bed and remembering how her mother was clean an entire year and a half before she met Cletus, how she started a program of self-improvement. She read all the time, self-help books she bought at yard sales, and she'd holler for Tiffany to come and listen to this or that passage in *I'm Okay, You're Okay* or *The Road Less Traveled*. She bought a copy of *Easy Rider* and made Tiffany watch it with her, it's a classic, she said, it came out ten years before Mom was born, and at the end they both cried and cried, watching Wyatt's body go flying over his motorcycle, and Mom's eyes had glinted with satisfaction, as though she had shown her some important lesson nobody else but Mom could teach.

Her chest rattles with a ragged sob, and she knows she looks like a fucking Goth with her black mascara all runny, but she can't stop sobbing, and Terry looks at her now, she has his undivided attention, even though he still has the cell phone curled to his ear. What the fuck is wrong with you? He's mad and he's demanding an answer, but she doesn't know. She holds her arms up in the air, flailing her hands in surrender, and he says I've got to go, I've got a situation, and puts the cell phone down, but she's already out of the car, stumbling into the dirt road, and Terry says, where the fuck do you think you're going? and grabs her elbow and pulls her roughly back toward the car.

She puts her arms around him, crying, trying to lay her head against his back, but he pulls her arms loose from around his waist, and says, it's too late for that, little girl, nothing sexy about a chick making a rough landing, but that isn't what she wants, not what he wants. She wants him to kiss her slowly and look her in the eye and say her name, say Tiffany, the way Dorothy says she wants to go home and clicks the heels of her red shoes.

But what happens is she starts puking into the dirt beside the car, puking and sobbing, and whirling her roughly around, he says, oh, Jesus, don't get any in the car.

He waits a minute to see if she's done. Then he pushes her into the seat and slams the door and gets in on the other side. Ought to fucking leave you out here, he says, let you walk home, and she thinks if she could just lie down and sleep, it would be all right, she wouldn't be any trouble, she could sleep right here on the ground.

Maybe she's a witch, like her mother, flying home on a broom, sailing over the mall and the subdivision where Terry lives in his own basement apartment in his mother and daddy's big stone house. People say they have a pool and a wide-screen TV and a white sofa in a room nobody goes in but company, but she doesn't know, she has never been there, she isn't in that crowd. She can feel how mad Terry is when he has to get out of the car and help her to the door of the trailer, and she's glad the door is unlocked because she doesn't think she could bend over to feel under the step and find the key.

She falls onto the sofa and he's gone, and she's cold but she's too drunk to get up and find a blanket. She dreams about water and her jeans are warm and then cold and she thinks she's peed on herself, but she can't get up to do anything about it because she's on a boat that's unsteady beneath her, and she can't afford to tip over and drown.

When she wakes up, she thinks it's raining, the rain dripping from the eaves, but it isn't rain, it's the roaches. She hears first one and then another drop from the ceiling to the kitchen counter. She doesn't keep the kitchen clean enough, Mom yells and yells, the roaches will take us over, we can't spray them, the spray would kill me, don't you care? Tiffany has never seen a roach during the day, but sometimes at night when she gets up for a drink of water, she finds them in the kitchen, sometimes scurrying for cover, and other times staying completely still, as if this will make them invisible.

The light flies on in the kitchen, hurting her eyes, and she hears Cletus's hand hit the counter. "Damn!" Then his shoe twisting on the linoleum. "Got you, you bastard!"

He turns the light out and comes into the living room. She closes her eyes and pretends to be sleeping, but when he comes and bends over her, she smells his breath, or is it hers? and she's sick again, drooping her head over the edge of the sofa, which is all she can manage right now.

He scrambles up and gets the throw from the recliner to catch the vomit, then puts his hand in front of her to keep her from rolling onto the floor. When she has finished, he takes the throw outside, and she hears the clang of the metal trash can lid, then Cletus's heavy step as he comes back into the trailer. She hears him down the hall, and tries to sit up. When he returns he is carrying a wash rag and one of Mom's white terry bathrobes, without any dye, the only kind she can wear.

He wipes her face, then reaches to pull off her blue top, and she lets him. Then he unbuttons her jeans and pulls them down, too, wiping her legs with the rag. Her head is pounding, but she manages to lift her butt, and then to stand, holding her arms out so he can slip them into the sleeves. The robe feels warm and Cletus ties the sash tight around her waist. He leads her down the hall to her bedroom and turns the bed down. Then he puts his arms around her for a moment and holds her against him.

He helps her into the bed, tucking her in tenderly, stroking her hair, and then his hand finds its way down the length of her body, settling the blanket around her as if he is spinning her into a cocoon. He lies down beside her and his hand lingers on her hip, but he doesn't go any further. Boys might go poking into her, make her go too fast, but he's her step daddy, see? He only wants what's best for her, to keep her warm and safe.

Doesn't he hear the bugs in the kitchen, dropping from the ceiling in the darkness? The man comes in his chemical suit to spray, she hears his truck outside, and struggles to get up, but her mother yells out the window for him to go away. Then her mother goes back to sleep, too, and Cletus comes to her bed and crawls in, but the man won't give up, he just comes around to the back of the trailer and bangs on the window, he will not take the hint. You'll be sorry, he says. You see one or two at night, you think you can just kill them, but think of the ones in the wall just waiting for their chance to come out. They won't hide then, will they? You'll never get rid of them. They'll be so brazen, they'll come right out in middle of the day.

She stirs, feeling a roach crawl across her shoulder, but it's just Cletus's hand patting her and she doesn't know which is worse. She tries to cry out, but she can't. Where is her mother? She tries to sit up, but her eyelids are like lead, and Cletus pulls her gently back down to the pillow, cradling her head in his hand. Shhh, he says. Shhh. Baby. You poor baby.

She feels the weight of his arm across her, and she wants to say I'm not Mom, I'm Tiffany, this is Tiffany, leave me alone, but the bed is spinning. She's dizzy and she wishes she was back little again, traveling with the carnival, getting a free ride to test the Tilt-a-Whirl before they let the crowds in. The gates open, and there's Terry, sauntering past the tents full of prizes that line the fairway. She waves, but she's whirling so fast she's invisible, strapped in the seat by herself.

Drug Therapy

You tell the doctor you're thinking about approaching the pharmaceutical industry and the government with a proposal to put antidepressants into the water supply. You say, don't you see how this could work? All those hearts that have been aching for years. All those desires exposed like fevered skin to frigid air. You could spark a new stage in humanity's evolution, with its own fossil history. As the drug enters the system, the crippled hearts will be silted like fern leaves or curled shells into layers of carbon, no longer fact, but artifacts, to be dug out in the future and examined through a magnifying glass for the stories they can tell.

You tell him how you see girls younger than you, longing tender on their faces, like an abrasion or a sunburn. You want to tell them, Wait. You want to say, this, too, shall pass. But what if it doesn't? And what if what passes leaves a space for something even worse? And that's why it's best just to have the drugs.

You tell him one of the first beneficiaries of your therapy should be Marty, the secretary of the English department. During the six years you've known her, Marty has lost a mother, a sister, an aunt. Over the years, she has imagined so many lumps in her own breasts that last week, when she found a real one, she wanted to laugh in disbelief. Except the doctor showed her on the X-ray.

Except it hasn't gone away.

But *your* doctor says, Wait and see. *Your* doctor says, sometimes these things turn out to be nothing. But Marty, like you, believes in Something, the Something she has been waiting for all her life. Think about it, you say, what she must have gone through: the women Marty loved most were carved up and stitched back, scarred as brides of Frankenstein. Her grandmother's hair fell out red and grew back in gray, but her straight-haired aunt got a free permanent wave, the chemicals applied not to the hair, but from inside the scalp, through the veins.

You tell the doctor he can be optimistic, but Marty knows it must be—no, you can see how she catches herself, every time. She won't finish the sentence, even in her mind. She thinks, it must be—and the blank she leaves is a stone so heavy at the center of her heart, she can't budge it with her lungs. You saw her try, in the women's bathroom the day she found the lump. Her breath came in shallow gasps, and you wondered if she would be able to take in enough air to keep herself alive long enough to die.

You tell the doctor about Bridget, the young girl in the office who comes in every morning with her head ducked down. Her eyes slice away from you, from the questions she imagines curled and waiting, like a scorpion's tail, at the tip of your tongue. She is in love with your lover, but she is invisible to him, as you were, until your anger made you real. When it started, she came to work every morning with her eyes shining, but you knew what she didn't. Now she comes in with her fragile self, her true self, tucked inside a suede coat so heavy, she bends over, wearing it. She looks like a peony with its petals brown at the edges, as though her head has grown too heavy for its narrow stem.

You should have warned her, you say. But your doctor says, just what makes you think you are the Mistress of the Universe. He says, are you trying to put him out of a job. He says, don't you have enough to worry about, with your own history of depression. Because that's what it is. You know that now. You have a Diagnosis. When he described your disease to you, you imagined your thoughts running like wild horses down the black diamond slopes of your mind, and you see how it is safer for everyone if they can corral them with cognitive therapy and a course of good drugs. You used to think you were sad, but sadness has gone out of existence. They cannot treat it.

You say, I'm serious. You ought to call somebody at Eli Lilly. You offer him your idea free of charge. After all, just look at what the drugs have done for you. Remember how for weeks you called your lover on his cell phone, at his office, at home, and when his wife answered, you hung up. You hated and loved the sick feeling you had at the pit of your stomach when you heard his voice, your power to strike fear in his heart, and even though he told you if you didn't stop, he was going to have to call a judge, a lawyer, your mother, you didn't believe him. Then he said he was going to put a stop to your craziness, once and for all. Even if he had hell to pay. Even if he had to tell the truth. And you knew then you had been right all along—you had a weapon you could wield again and again. Because no matter how much he blustered and raved at you, you knew you could not take his threats seriously. Because he isn't capable of honesty. Because he isn't capable of paying anything at all.

Then, a month later, when you picked up the receiver, the phone heavy in your hand, you couldn't imagine calling anybody. It was too much trouble to remember his arms wrapped around you, his lies falling against your ear, burying you in the silence of your desire, until there was nothing but your heart beating, the despair and joy driving you toward the surface rhythmic as a swimmer's frantic hands. For weeks you had to play dead at the bottom of the pool, and if there was a face peering down into the blue water to look for you, you had trouble recognizing the features through the distortion of the sunlight and gallons and gallons of water that pressed your weighted body down.

You remind the doctor how before the drugs you used to go to bed at night with a bird trapped in the dark chimney of your heart. Now, you sleep the sleep of the dead, who no longer even have to worry about their dreams.

So, of course, you are so much better now. He's made you a believer, and you don't see why anybody needs to be miserable in this day and time. Think of Hamlet, you say, if he'd had Prozac. Maybe he would have stopped all that whining. Maybe he'd have been able to make up his mind.

You tell him how just this morning, you waited in the line at Kroger behind a young mother. She had one child on her hip and tugged another along by the hand. In front of you was an old man in a white shirt, yellowed like parchment, his pants too short and held around his waist by suspenders. The mother had on pink sweat pants and a shirt that left a gap between her waistband and her pale skin. When she took the wadded bills out of her pocket to pay for her groceries, for a second you wanted to—what? Your new self laughs at the old self who sometimes still has this crazy urge to save the world. Did you want to stock her pantry? Baby-sit her children? Take her home to raise? And she's just one lonely woman on a planet full of them. It's like one of those movies set in a war zone. People keep coming and coming, running onto the tarmac, but there's only this one small plane.

The old man was frail and reminded you of your grandfather. Of everybody's grandfather, the doctor says, as if he was there with you, as if he thinks he's a ventriloquist in your brain, as if, without him to interpret, you don't have sense enough to know what you mean.

You wrinkle your nose, playing along. You say the old man

reeked of stale tobacco smoke and sweat, and by the way has the doctor ever observed that sweaty armpits smell just like ground cumin? He laughs and says, now you've ruined tonight's dinner at Mia Casita, and he's been looking forward to it all day.

This is when you begin again to hide things from him. You do not tell him that you're tempted to write a letter to your lover's wife telling her everything, or that you might just send a Xeroxed copy to Bridget, which she can take or leave.

You certainly do not say that the old man's odor reminded you of death. Or that, when you turned your head away from his tragic and unspeakable ruin, in spite of the drugs that have made you healthy and realistic, the drugs that have been your salvation, you could not help but feel ashamed.

The Baby

In the heat of the afternoon, Mamaw takes away the cane-bottomed chairs that prop the doors to the rag store open, and they sit together on the wide front porch, hoping for a breeze from the river.

In the shade at the far end, Grampa moves the green and white steel glider back and forth, rocking himself to sleep. The rusty metal skreaks, but softly, like crickets from far off. Mamaw wears a printed cotton dress the color of the mixed impatiens that grow by the broken bottom porch steps, and Alice Ann sits on the top step next to Mamaw, the girl's face dark and flat as a spatter of mud.

Alice Ann's mother died two years before, when she was six, and since then she has carried herself more like an old woman than a child, her head drooping forward, top-heavy like a sunflower, her shoulders rounded and hunched. Her dark hair grows in a widow's peak framing her wide white forehead. She is staying with Mamaw and Grampa while her daddy's up north somewhere, looking for a job.

Mamaw squints into the sunlight.

"What?" Alice Ann says, because Mamaw has her head tilted as though she is listening for something.

"Hear it? Sounds like a baby, don't it? Crying. From somewhere far off?"

Alice Ann tilts her head, too, to see if she can hear it. Mamaw often hears things before anybody else does—the hiss of a rattler in the blackberry briars, the rumble of thunder from a storm a day away. Sometimes Grampa goes behind the store and makes noises just to fool her, trying to make her think the clothes in the store are full of crickets or that there's a whippoorwill calling out death in the middle of the day. But being smarter than Grampa she hardly ever falls for his tricks. When she does, he rides her about it for a week or two. At supper, between bites, he'll make the sound again, laughing so hard that sometimes he chokes on his food and has to call for her to bring him a glass of water.

She always brings it, and Alice Ann bends to feed a bite of her chicken to the cat rubbing her leg beneath the table, ashamed to see Mamaw, who has more sense in her little finger than Grampa has in his whole body, wait on him like he's king of the hill. Alice Ann, who has gone straight from the third grade to the fifth because her teacher says she can read words high school graduates can't, is smarter than either one of them, though she knows Mamaw is wise. When she grows up, she'll kill somebody before she'll let him treat her the way Grampa treats Mamaw. She'll just get her a gun, aim it, and shoot straight at his heart.

But today, Grampa is just snoring, and Mamaw picks up Sammy, her little grandbaby, who lies on the porch next to her and Alice Ann. She lifts his hands, and he laughs, spit bubbling down his chin. His head is covered with sparse white hair, fine and wispy as baby chick feathers. Sammy started trying to sit up early, but his big head weighs him down. His mother, Alice Ann's Aunt Brenda, took him to a doctor, but he told her not to worry. All babies start out this way, and sooner or later, the rest of Sammy will grow to match the size of his head. But even now, when the baby is learning to walk, to get up he has to roll over first from the flat of his back and use his fat little arms for leverage.

Mamaw rolls up the baby's undershirt and bends to blow on his belly. "I got you," she says, and Sammy kicks his little feet and laughs.

The wind catches the tail of Mamaw's red dress, and she pulls it tight to cover the tops of the thick support stockings she wears rolled to the base of her knees. She sits upright and leans against the gray post behind her, narrowing her eyes as she studies the heat that hangs between the store and river.

"It's just a bird or something you heard," Alice Ann says. She doesn't want to contradict Mamaw, but she has listened for five whole minutes and hasn't heard a thing.

"I don't know what it was, but it wasn't no bird." She picks up Sammy's feet and holds them in her big, freckled hands, pulling them close enough to her face to give the heels a kiss. "I'm telling you, there's another baby somewhere around here," she answers, not looking at Alice Ann, and bicycles Sammy's fat legs in her hands. "I heard it crying right after we moved in. At first I didn't think it could be a baby, either, thought it was maybe an old cat squalling, but I reckon I know a baby crying when I hear one. Sometimes of a night it just cries and cries. I've looked everywhere for it. I tracked it to the corner of the loft once, but then it sounded like it was coming from the front of the house. It always comes from some place where at the time I ain't looking."

A rag of cloud covers the sun for a minute, and, shivering, Alice Ann presses her face into the soft material of Mamaw's dress. She feels dizzy from the heat, and she wonders if maybe she's about to have a sunstroke. Mamaw said one of her old aunts had a sunstroke and died of it. She was hoeing between the tomato plants in her garden right at noon, and when her husband came home from the mines to eat dinner, after looking everywhere for

69

her, he found her dead, flat on her back, in between the rows.

"I don't care to tell you, first time I heard it crying, it nearly scared the ticking out of me, but I couldn't keep from looking for it anyway. Grampa said I was about to run him crazy, up and down all night. He had all but decided to tell Ed Jenkins we didn't want this place no more, he couldn't stand it, when it stopped. It was the pitch black of midnight, so dark you couldn't see your hand stretched out in front of your face. I had my flashlight out from under the bed and my feet on the floor, when it give a little jerking sound, like it was all wore out with crying, and then it just quit. That's why it startled me, a minute ago, for I hadn't heard a peep out of it since."

Alice Ann looks down at Sammy. Grampa says Mamaw's got a screw loose somewhere, that's why she hears things, and Alice Ann hates to side with him against her, but she thinks that must be true. "Ain't no babies around here but Sammy," she says, her voice muffled against Mamaw's sleeve. "Maybe he cries of a night and you hear him?"

Mamaw shakes her head. "Him and his Mama live three miles up the holler from here. Sound don't carry that far. And there could be a baby here." She does look at Alice Ann now, to make sure she's listening. "Ed told me right after we first come back down here from Cleveland that a farmer a mile or so up had a girl to get in trouble. She was fat anyhow, so she was real far along before her people knowed for sure something was wrong. Ed, he figures it was a trucker got her that way, one that used to stop by his store for a baloney sandwich and a carton of milk when he come this way hauling coal."

Mamaw rolls Sammy over and lays her wide, flat hand on the baby's back. The sun is pale yellow like a dollop of butter and has dropped so low in the sky that it nearly rests on the top of the mountain. A hot wind blows down the hollow, kicking up red dust

70

and turning the maple leaves over until their undersides shine like dimes.

"When the girl's daddy found out she was in a family way, he said he'd take a stick to her. I reckon he scared her so bad she snuck off somewhere. Ed said she was gone two weeks before her daddy told anybody, hoping she'd run off with the truck driver."

"Was that what happened?" Alice Ann asks. "Did she run off with him?" She swats a mosquito and then hitches up her blue jeans to scratch at a bite on the back of her calf, digging with her fingernails until it starts to bleed.

"Quit it," Mamaw says, slapping Alice's hand away. "You look like you got small pox, you got so many of them scabs. Honey, that man had two kids already. He was long gone before that girl even knowed to go looking for him. Anyway, just hush and let me tell it. Because, you see, what happened is, the girl died. She was near dead already when they found her. Place was empty then, and Ed had come over here to set out some rat poison. She was in that room back of the store here, and Ed said he heard a whimpering sound. She was laying on an old blue tarpaulin, shivering, all soaked with blood. Ed put her in the back of his pickup and carried her up the road to her daddy's. I reckon her daddy liked to have killed Ed when he seen her, but Ed finally calmed him. Anybody with any sense could look at Ed and see he didn't do nothing to her, he's harmless as an old shoe."

"What about the baby?" Alice Ann waits for an answer, tearing the scab off a mosquito bite on the inside of her ankle and pressing her finger hard against it to make it sting. "Did she have the baby with her?"

"No," Mamaw says. "That's the mystery of it. They never found no baby."

"It's dead," Alice Ann says. "Of course, it would be."

"Might be. But tell me this—how come they never found its

little body?"

Alice Ann thinks about it. Mamaw has a point. If you don't have a body, you can't have a funeral. Her own mother had died in the county hospital after a bad wreck, but Alice Ann did not believe it, she was inconsolable. But then they had the funeral, and she could see how her mother was so still she had to be dead. She cried every night for her mother for a long time after, but now her mother seems like somebody she saw on a TV show or met in a dream. It's her daddy she misses. She expects him to come down here every day and get her. She wakes up every morning wishing her daddy will be standing by the couch she sleeps on, and then she can finally decide whether to hug his neck or to refuse to speak to him until he's been home a week or more, to punish him for going away.

"Ed figures some homeless people got it," Mamaw says. "He says they used to sleep in the back room where she had it. They'd pee on the floor and leave worse in a drywall bucket, and one time, he found that old Warm Morning stove scooted clear over to the window. They'd stuck the stovepipe out, busted up one of his grandma's dining chairs for kindling, and lit her up. Wonder they didn't burn the whole place down."

"I bet it was dead, and they buried it."

"Didn't find a trace of a grave, neither. Now, Ed figures they took it down there and drowned it."

Alice Ann studies the thick vines that hide the river, making it eerie and full of mystery. Even the light there has a green tint to it. She has found all kinds of stuff washed up on the bank—a Swiss army knife with some of the blades missing, a ruby-colored ring wrapped with twine to fit her middle finger, and an army hat too big for her head that makes her feel like she's a giant turtle. One time she wore the helmet to bed, and she dreamed she was riding in a railroad car, one ear pressed tight against the floor where she could hear the wheels pounding against the rails. A real train was passing back of the house, and she felt the floor tremble under her, and when she woke up, the helmet was pushed almost to her shoulders and Grampa loomed over the bed, pounding the helmet with his palms.

She shivers, thinking of finding a baby on the bank, still and dead. "Looks like it would have floated," she says, thinking of the roundness of a baby and the strength of the water, the way it makes even her narrow body weightless, pushing her to the top. Sometimes, when the pool of shallow water above the bridge is thick with bluegill, she lies beside the river on her stomach, dropping bread in the water and watching the fish dart up from the cold muddy bottom, nibbling until every last crumb is gone.

"Here. Take him for a minute," Mamaw says, laying Sammy across Alice Ann's lap. She wishes she could find a baby. She knows how to take care of one. When Sammy was even smaller, right after his mother, Alice Ann's aunt, started working at Palm Beach and had to leave him with Mamaw, Alice Ann had held him all the time, cradling his hand in the crook of her arm, careful not to touch his soft spot where the scalp sinks in like the stem end of a cantaloupe.

Grampa is awake and walking to their end of the porch, yawning and stretching. He has a round chest, his belly spilling over his belt, but his arms and legs are spindly. He looks like a picture of Humpty Dumpty Alice Ann saw once in a Little Golden Book, but he can move fast. Sometimes on Sundays he plays tag with Alice Ann and her cousins. He takes out his partial plate and finger-brushes his hair to stand up on the top of his head where it sticks out like the feathers of some huge, white combed rooster. Then, lurching from side to side, he chases them around the store. Alice Ann is smarter than her cousins, and she doesn't let him catch her. She has learned that Grampa goes after the ones that think they can outrun him, and she can make herself so still, she can hide in plain sight.

It isn't good to let him catch you. When he wins, he'll wrestle you to the floor tickling and pinching, rubbing his whiskers against your face until they're red as fire. If you cry, he says, Baby, Big Baby. One or two of her aunts by marriage won't let their kids play with him anymore, but his own girls sit on the front porch drinking iced tea as if they don't know a thing in the world is wrong.

Mamaw always carries hard candy in her pocket, butterscotch or peppermint, and she'll give them to the children to make them feel better. "Here, now. Don't cry," she'll say, wiping their snotty noses with the hem of her apron. "You don't want him to mess with you, you don't have to play."

Alice Ann draws away when he comes toward her and Sammy. She looks around for Mamaw, but Mamaw is in the garden picking them a tomato or two for supper, her back turned away. By now the sun has melted completely behind the rim of the mountain, dark yellow like piece of butterscotch candy

She tries to hold on to Sammy when Grampa leans over to pick him up, but this is silly, like something out of Solomon. This is his own grand baby, what's she supposed to do, hold on until one of them pulls the baby in two? He plays a little rough is all, but she still sucks her breath in when Grampa turns Sammy upside and swings him back and forth by his heels. Sammy squeals with laughter at first, but then, dangling upside down, his cheeks turn red and he starts to howl.

Alice Ann stands up, reaching for the baby. She cups her hand at the crown of Sammy's big head, afraid that if Grampa holds the baby this way for very long, the weight of Sammy's head might pull it loose from his neck, and it will bounce right down the porch steps and roll all the way to the river.

Alice Ann lifts herself to her elbows and lies very still, listening, hoping to hear the baby again. But the only sound she recognizes is the hiss of Grampa's cigarette. He sits across the room from her. She can see the red coal burning where his mouth should be, can make out the shape of him, his undershirt a white U, the rest of him disappearing into the darkness. He often roams through their rooms at night, his pale flat feet slapping softly against the cold linoleum floor. Sometimes Alice Ann wakes up startled to find him at the foot of the couch she sleeps on, wide awake and looking at her.

She scoots up from the sofa, rubbing her eyes. The blanket drops from her shoulders. "Did you hear it?"

The cigarette hisses and glows. "Hear what?"

A cloud scoots past the moon, and Grampa's shirt dims and brightens. Alice Ann leans back against the arm of the couch and laces her hands behind her head. She doesn't want to fall back to sleep, not while Grampa is up, and there is still a chance she might hear the baby. She thinks of all the places somebody might hide it—in the wall? Maybe the mother hid it in the wall to keep the homeless people from getting it? Or somewhere in the weeds that grow thick by the river, the way Moses' mother hid Moses in the bulrushes, leaving Miriam on the bank to watch.

A breeze flutters the curtains behind the chair where Grampa sits smoking, and the three-quarter moon hangs low over the ridgeline, tilted down like a woman's face. Mamaw says on nights like this the curtains look like girls in white nightgowns, dancing for the moon. Tonight the moon looks so close that Alice Ann lifts her hand without thinking, as if she could just reach out into the sky and touch the woman's cheek.

Her head drops back against the pillow, and the chair creaks as

Grampa shifts his weight. She is tired of lying on her back, but she doesn't want to roll onto her side, afraid the pillow will muffle the sound of the baby if it cries again. When she finds the baby, she will let it sleep with her, on the inside, where it won't fall out.

It would be hers, wouldn't it, if she found it? And she must have asked this aloud, because Grampa's cigarette hisses and glows and he says, "Finders keepers, losers, weepers."

The next day is Tuesday, bundle day. Every Tuesday, a truck brings a load of bundles full of used clothes to the store. Mamaw pays a flat rate of three dollars each, which she says is too high, but, still, selling each piece for a nickel or a dime—good clothes, like a winter coat, might bring fifty or seventy-five cents—she makes a big profit, even though she never goes anywhere to buy anything for herself.

Once Alice Ann caught Mamaw hiding a five-pound coffee can full of money under a loose plank in the smokehouse. Mamaw was on her knees, using a butter knife to pry up the plank. When she looked up at Alice Ann, she had looked startled, then her face relaxed, and she motioned Alice Ann to shut the door.

"What's his is his, and what's mine is his," she whispered, emptying her pockets and mashing the bills on top down with her hand. "You can keep a secret, can't you?" Alice Ann had nodded, staring down at Mamaw' clutching the can full of money to her chest, her thick finger nails outlined with dirt, ashamed to know a secret that had the power to make Mamaw so afraid.

They have a big crowd of women on Tuesdays, and Mamaw slits the bundles open with her pocketknife, to show that the clothes haven't already been picked through. The bright contents spill out in the middle of the dusty wood floor, and the women sit cross-legged on the floor and pick through the used clothes, looking for a bargain. Why, look how rich people throw clothes away with their tags still on!

Tuesday is Mamaw's day to gossip and barter, better than any of her soap operas on TV, and while she is occupied, Alice Ann sneaks down to the water. Mamaw hates the water. She won't let Alice Ann go down there, warning her about a girl years ago who didn't even swim, just *dipped her feet in!* and was sucked into a hole and drowned. But Alice Ann loves the river, and goes down there whenever she can slip away. Even on the hottest days, the leaves and vines grow so thick it is dark and cool there, and the light is a gold-green color, like a secret world. On flat rocks at the water's low point, skinks, tails electric blue and quivering, rest in the sunlight.

Today, all Alice Ann can think about is the baby. *Her* baby. If she were to hide a baby, she thinks this is where she would put it. That way, if it got thirsty, it could turn over and get a drink, and it could eat the way the fish did, nibbling at breadcrumbs that float by.

This late in summer, the soil next to the river is hard and dry. Crumbled sandstone, her daddy told her. They walked down here the day before he left Kentucky to go and look for work in the city, and he had pointed to the cliff face downstream where the water fanned out. Look, he said. See how the lines dividing the rocks just stop and then start up again, a little higher up. That's a fault line, he told her. A long time ago, there was an earthquake here. When he came back, he would teach her all about how to read the rocks, the whole history of the world was in them. Alice Ann looked, but all she saw was the shape of an angel, one wing dipped toward the water, and the face had been sanded away. He had squeezed her shoulder. "They're your mama's people," he said. "It's better like this."

In a shady spot where the water pools, Alice Ann takes a stick and swishes it through the leaves. And then, she hears it. From a thicket of scrub brush smothered in vines, she hears first a low whimpering sound, then a high-pitched wail. Wah! Wah! Wah!

She scrambles up and heads toward the sound, but it's just the way Mamaw said. Every time she gets close to where she thinks the sound is coming from, it moves just a little piece away. She starts and stops, following, head cocked and listening.

Just beyond a boulder, caught in a pocket of muddy water, floats a baby's rattle. Alice Ann kneels in the sharp stone and strains to reach it. The rattle is round, with a hook on the end, and the top, which looks as though it used to be red, has faded to a dull pink the color of a tongue.

Alice Ann uses the stick to pull the rattle toward her, and just as she grabs it, she hears a step. She stands and turns, holding the rattle behind her, to hide it.

"What did you find?" Grampa says, softly, as if he is asking her to share a secret, even though they are far away from the rag store, and there is nobody around to hear.

"Nothing."

"Let me see your hand."

She looks up at him, and even though she knows he is not very tall, standing on the bank a few feet above her, he looks gigantic. Behind her, toward the house, the water curves and narrows, and the trees on both banks lean toward each other, tangling their leaves. She shakes her head and starts around him, but he catches her up, fastening her legs around his waist. His chest is hot and damp, and he smells like sweat and cigarettes. She loses the rattle, and twists her head to see where it dropped, but he takes her chin hard in his hand and pulls her face around, lowering his own into her line of vision. His mouth is open, and his breath smells bad, like rotted weeds, and something in his eyes that she doesn't understand but that scares her makes her jerk her head away, hard, wiggling, and pushing away from him with her arms.

She pushes so hard that when he lets go, he drops her, and she scrambles up and away. She half runs and half crawls up the rocky hillside, catching her hands and hair on the briars, scraping across the rocks with her knees. At the top, she hesitates, looking back to see if he is behind her. He is still there, but he isn't bothering to chase her. He doesn't have to. He knows where she is, and he has all the time in the world.

When he sees her look back, he cups his hands around his mouth and makes the sound, Wah! Wah! Wah! And then he laughs so hard the laughter shakes him to his knees and he beats his palms on the ground.

She's sick and Mamaw keeps feeling of her head, but she doesn't have a fever. It's her heart, it's heavy as a stone. Last night, she dreamed somebody came and laid a rock on her chest, or was it her grave? It was hot inside, and her mouth was covered with moisture where the rain had seeped through, but she turned into a black bird and flew away to perch on the curtain rod and when she looked down he was on top of her trying to suck out her breath, but ha ha! she's up here, small and far away, and she flew right out the window, beating her black wings, following the curve of the river to the wide, wide sea.

Mamaw wants her to come in, out of the damp, she'll catch her death. But Alice Ann thinks she will stay out here forever on the little side porch at the top of the stairs. Mamaw comes out and wraps a quilt around Alice Ann's shoulders and sits down on the top step beside her.

The night is cool for August, and Alice Ann takes Mamaw's hand and puts it under the quilt to warm it. Under the quilt, Mamaw reaches in her pocket, and Alice Ann takes the candy. She unwraps it and puts it in her mouth, salt and its buttery sweetness melting slow against her tongue. She is glad to have the candy and not to have to talk. They both know what they know, but neither of them wants to be the one to say.

Under the bridge the wind knocks Ed Jenkins' little fishing boat against the pilings, and the ropes whine as the front of the boat strains to break free. She thinks of taking Mamaw with her and stealing the boat. Alice Ann could do all the rowing, while Mamaw sits in the back, her hair in two gray braids falling over her shoulder like an Indian queen's. But Mamaw is afraid of the water, she wouldn't go, and Alice Ann is still little, only eight, and she's afraid to go alone.

Clouds clot across the stars, thick with rain, and the wind catches in the tops of the trees. It sounds like a baby crying, and Alice Ann turns her head to listen for a second before she remembers that there is no baby, there are no babies allowed in this house, their heads are so filled up with dread they weigh too much for their little necks to hold them. Any babies around here, if they're going to make it, have to grow up fast and learn to run. The only babies are in the stories, whirling around her, and you think they're telling secrets, but they're hiding secrets, too.

Working Sketches

Philip lies on his back, smoking. The tendrils of smoke drift toward the ceiling, where a dove gray haze hovers above us. Through the smoke the cracked plaster looks like the background of an antique photograph. The only thing missing is the face.

Philip's arm is flung over his eyes to shade them from the light that pierces the slit in the blue-flowered curtains. I sit next to him lotus-style, my knees touching his warm skin, fanning my fingers through the hair that grows in the valley between his ribs. He is short, barrel-chested, and when I hook my index finger in his belly button, the first joint of it disappears.

He stirs and fumbles on the nightstand for his watch. "I have to go."

Because this is his secondary, not primary, relationship, I reply with resignation, "I know."

But he hesitates after he snaps his watchband into place, lying there long enough to trace the curve of my left breast. "Do you realize that until I met you I had never made love to a woman with freckles on her breasts?"

"You make love, but you don't love. Dearest, that's a paradox," I observe, which is the closest I ever come to criticism.

Even at that small barb, Philip lifts my hand from his belly and shuts the fingers. Then he swings around the edge of the bed, digging underneath the dust ruffle for his shoes. He sighs, long and whooshing, like a tire deflating when its plug is pulled. "Sally, if I loved anyone besides Gloria or our daughter, it would be you."

Philip is a psychologist, a marriage counselor, and he says that years of listening to neurotic people talk about their bad relationships has robbed him of the concept of fidelity. "Skinner was right about one thing," he tells me every so often, forgetting he read me the same thing, sentence by sentence, from a paper he wrote last year for a conference. "When it comes to our physical needs at least, we're stimulus-response creatures. We see food and we salivate. Between the legs, it's the same."

Philip and I work in the same building. His office is on the third floor, and I do title searches for an attorney on the second. I met him at noon on a park bench outside. He says he stood there for ten minutes, watching me crumble my toasted cheese sandwich and feed the pieces to the birds that glided down from the sky in slow motion to peck around my feet. "I had an intense feeling of déjà vu," he says. "Maybe even an image from another life: a freckled girl in a white ruffled blouse, feeding pigeons."

I like my work, even if sometimes it's tedious. I like the idea that everything is recorded somewhere, that you can trace the provenance of land back, even though technically I'm only checking to see there are no outstanding mortgages.

What I really am is an artist, so I guess you could say that when I'm not tracing the legal records of land, I'm trying myself to record it. I paint. No the muted landscapes that my mother always favored, but huge canvasses filled with leaves that bulge as if their veins are swollen with liquid—very sexy, Philip says, like vulvas—suns that spill over the ridges of mountains like broken egg yolks. My apartment is one big mural. What were once basic white walls are now all kinds of forests—tropical forests and redwood forests and evergreen forests and primeval forests--each with lush undergrowth of fern. Philip says that when we are eating dinner, he can almost feel the sprinkle of sap.

Philip has one child, a daughter he and Gloria adopted from an orphanage in Romania. Once when I smuggled a picnic supper up to his office after hours, we ate sub sandwiches, and he showed me a photograph album that chronicled their lives since she had arrived. He speaks of the girl, Maria, glowingly, of her improved English, her gratitude at being rescued, her European reserve. But I can't help noticing that in the pictures of himself and Gloria at the airport, Gloria is holding little Maria by the hand, but he stands a little away from them, and he cannot quite bring himself to smile.

Dark and thin, Maria could be Gloria's by birth. Now that Maria is away at college, Gloria teaches yoga and dance at night at a local fitness center in addition to her tenure-track position teaching sociology at a community college. One Sunday afternoon, I saw her shopping with Philip, but for obvious reasons, he didn't acknowledge me, and I walked right on, headed to the movies by myself. She is beautiful, much prettier than I am. She coils her long dark hair into a bun at the nape of her long neck, and a widow's peak turns her ivory face into a heart. That Sunday she wore an emerald silk blouse that flowed around her body like water. Her movements were so fluid that when she walked past me, the delicatessen, Spencer's gifts, and the Appalachian crafts store, I wanted to paint her dancing.

Philip is teaching me to get in touch with my body. I told him that I took an education course once where the instructor's favorite method of getting the students acquainted was to make us turn sideways, massage each other's shoulders, and "rain" on each other's heads. We rained by making light little typing strokes with our fingers. While everybody else was breaking the ice, I sat down, and the teacher came by and encouraged me, but I wouldn't do it, and the next day I dropped the class. 'I don't like to be touched,' I told him."

Now Philip rains on me all the time, and not just the top of my skull, and I love it. He thinks he has cured me, but when a stranger looks at me too long on the street, I come home so wired up I have to drink a glass of wine. I still hold my elbows tight to my body in crowds, claustrophobic, and I cannot wait to get out into the fresh air.

Later in the afternoon, I call him at work, even though he has cautioned against it. He thinks he is so smooth, but when he says, "Just couldn't bear it any longer, could you, Melinda Potter?" I know he wants me. I imagine his receptionist listening on the other side of the closed door, knowing everything, because of course loves me so much he cannot keep hiding it forever.

Today, as always, I identify myself as Melinda Potter because she might know Sally Hatterman who works at Southeast Title, and Melinda Potter was once a bona fide patient of Philip's, a big, raw-boned woman he couldn't possibly be sleeping with, even if she hadn't moved to Bloomington, Indiana.

"You aren't with someone, are you?" I ask, though I know she would never have put me through if he had a client.

"I'm sorry I was so abrupt with you this morning," he says, "but I knew Gloria's plane would be in at ten, and even if I didn't have to rush off for a session—"

"Don't worry about it." This is part of the deal. I am not to get my feelings hurt. Gloria is Philip's primary relationship, and he needs time physically and emotionally to adjust from being with me to being with her. It's not just a shower to wash the sex off, but a whole reorientation of his attention.

"I wouldn't have called, but you did leave in a hurry. I didn't have time to tell you. I won't be here Thursday. We'll have to reschedule."

"We can't reschedule." Gloria teaches a class on Thursday, and if we don't get together then it will be Tuesday of next week, and even though Philip hates to wait that long to see me, he will almost never deviate from this schedule. Last night was a bonus because Gloria was out of town, but even then he was nervous, as if she might decide to come home on a whim. "Anyway, why do we need to reschedule? Is something wrong?"

"My grandmother is sick. Cancer. I haven't seen her in a long time. They're willing to give me some days off at work, and my mother wants me to come home."

He doesn't say anything for a moment, and I wait for him to say what people say, that he is so sorry, can he do anything? But he is Philip, so of course he doesn't do things the way other people do them, that would be a cliché, and I know I shouldn't, but I feel disappointed when he just says, "Oh. Well, we might be able to get together Saturday if you're back early. Gloria is going out to dinner with the other instructors at the gym. I was going to try and get some work done, but—"

"Of course. If I'm able to get back. Whenever you can work me in."

When I am away from Philip, I remember him in fragments— a wrinkled earlobe, his eyes the color of cured tobacco leaves, his leg nestled between mine like a spontaneously generated limb, a starfish's sixth appendage. Sometimes I try to conjure him up whole so that I can draw him, but all I come up with is a chin. The upper part of his face is like a mountain concealed in a bank of clouds.

I have my sketchpad out when my six-year-old niece asks me

to draw her picture. Her blue eyes are wide apart like mine with pale red lashes. When I finish, I tear off the page and give it to her, and she runs to show my brother.

"When are you going to get married and have some babies?" my uncle Ed asks, smiling. I have eaten and eaten until I have to unbutton the waistband of my jeans to breathe. I haven't done this in a long time, but I am so miserable I go to the bathroom, poke two fingers down my throat, and make myself throw up.

I draw the whole three days I'm home. I study my grandmother and make working sketches of what she will look like dead—her face framed by satin the color of lilies, head hollow as a Faberge egg; my mother staring past her bed at the window beaded up with rain. I don't last until Saturday. I leave Friday evening at twilight.

My mother hugs me before I leave, and for once I hold on so long, it is she who breaks the embrace, looking at me peculiarly and unfastening my arms from around her shoulders as though my hands were the clasp of a necklace.

She is still standing in the driveway, watching me back the car. I can see her in my rearview mirror until the last curve before the main highway, and then she's gone.

Saturday I paint deserts, but they don't satisfy me. They look like pictures of pictures, as if I were a precocious high school student copying Georgia O'Keefe. I wonder if my father is still living in Arizona. He loved me when I was too little to be a woman, my body like an Arizona desert, hairless and empty of hills.

After Philip and I make love, I go to the kitchen to make coffee. As I drop the measured scoops into the basket, Philip steps behind me, still naked, wrapping his arms around my waist, and I lean into his warmth. He has been quiet all afternoon. I remember my father being exactly the same way right before he left my mother. He stood on the walk at the foot of our gray wooden steps, the car running in the driveway. "Don't hate me," he said, but I sat huddled on the porch swing a few feet away, worrying at a splinter with my finger, unable to say the words that would release him from his misery.

Philip nuzzles my hair with his cheek. "I don't know what I'm going to do about you, Sally." The statement lingers in the air like a question.

"Yes, you do, Philip," I say finally, releasing him. "You know."

"Don't do it too fast," I caution. "I like it better slow."

He grins, a farm boy with lean arms and sky blue eyes. "I'll do it any way you like," he says, laying his cap on the nightstand. He's grinning as though he can't believe his luck, but he's embarrassed, too. "Are you sure?" he says, but I don't say anything at all.

I grill us cheese sandwiches for supper, and we do it again. "You are so pretty," he says, as I lead him to the sofa. "I mean, I just said hello because I thought you were waiting for somebody. I didn't want anybody to bother you. I never thought you'd—"

Any minute, I think, he's going to say gosh darn, and to keep him from spoiling things, I lay my hand across his lips. I push him gently back. Then I straddle him and undo the one button that fastens his plaid flannel shirt across my breasts. Closing my eyes, I think how simple it is. It isn't supposed to mean anything. Only boring, bourgeoisie people think it's supposed to mean something.

He settles against the pillow and sighs, and just as I hear the doorknob turn, I pause for a moment to drum lightly on his belly with my fingers. I am composing a picture for Philip to see when he walks through the door, a picture of me and this sweet farmer, making rain.

Houses

My mother lives with a man named Jerry, a carpenter, and on Saturdays he likes to take us to look at houses he is helping to build. A house he is very proud of, a three-story chalet rooted into a hillside, lies eight miles from the trailer park where we live.

Without the wallboard up, the house looks like a skeleton guarded by stacks of concrete blocks and pyramids of fieldstone. A two-by-ten sticks out of the doorway like a tongue. We use it to cross the narrow trench filled with gravel and drain tile.

At the entrance to what will become the kitchen, Jerry stands underneath the header and leans his hip against a cluster of two-by-fours. "You can't tell it now," he says, "but this house has almost 4,000 square feet."

He explains that houses look bigger the more you close them in. Sometimes they look so small with just the footers poured that people complain to the builder, afraid he picked up the wrong blueprint on the way to the site.

Jerry lights a heater in the middle of the room. Waving his thick hand in the air, he points out the quality of materials and workmanship. He says that the ten-inch oak beams that span the cathedral ceiling will still be there when we're all dead and rotting. This house will outlast us all.

Even with the heater turned up full blast, Ginny, my mother, stands with her hands shoved deep into the pockets of her parka. Wind gusts between the studs, stirring the leaves and trash that litter the floor. Ginny stoops to pick up a beer can that rolls in a half-circle, but Jerry stops her with his hand on her arm. Every so often, he says, the men sweep all the trash outside. When the bulldozer comes later to fill in around the basement and level the stacks of red mud, its blade will bury everything.

On the way home, Ginny sits with her nose pressed against the window, her narrow face pale in the dull November light. Jerry turns up the radio without looking at it. Willie Nelson sings a song about a man tougher than leather who kills a girl's sweetheart and then dies in despair because he has broken her heart.

"You can't break a heart," I say. Jerry looks at me in the rearview mirror as though I've sprung out of nowhere and haven't been with them all this time. "It's a pump. That's all your heart is. It looks like a tough piece of meat."

Jerry frowns, glancing sideways at my mother. Her eyes never leave the stream of hillsides dotted with trees and cows, the stretches of pastureland where white rocks jut out like pieces of old bone.

He takes her hand and kisses it. "I tell you what I'm gonna do," he says, letting go of her, watching her cross her legs and lace her fingers together over her left knee. "One of these days I'm gonna build us a house. Would you like that?"

While he talks, his hands hop on and off the steering wheel like a row of birds.

My mother was the only one in her family ever to go to college. The first time she went, she stayed only a semester. When she came home at Christmas, she was pregnant with me. This is all I know about my father: a thin-faced boy in a school picture, his wire-rimmed glasses riding low on the bridge of his nose; the same boy in a Polaroid snapshot, sitting on the hood of a white Mustang fastback, a red bandana tied pirate-style over his shoulder-length hair; some charcoal sketches Ginny made of him right before he got drafted. She says they don't really look like him. She could never get the right expression in his eyes.

I wanted to write to him a couple of times, but Ginny says she has no idea where to find him, that maybe he was killed in combat or what changed from the boy she remembers to someone beyond recognition. For years I imagined him plugged into us like a diver in a Jacques Cousteau special on educational TV. I can almost see him swaying at the end of a long, black line, while his eyes, like the lens of a camera, record for us the colors of fishes swimming around him in flashes of light.

Once at Christmas I saw a soldier in the Greyhound station. He wore a beret pulled low across his forehead. His glasses slipped a little as he bent over a paperback three inches thick. The round toes of his combat boots pointed at right angles, as if to keep a watch out for enemies coming both ways.

For a long time after that, I knew the times for incoming buses from Louisville. Unless a bus pulled in during school or the middle of the night, I was there to meet it. I sat at the counter eating greasy French fries, studying the face of every male passenger who turned sideways to lug a suitcase through the door.

In fact, the first time I saw Jerry sprawled across the sofa, the light from the window turning his short beard yellow as corn, I thought that my father had come home.

೫೦೧೩

Two weeks later, we visit the house again. Jerry slams the car door behind him and then waits to help Ginny up the hill. "Looks like the stonemason's been working this morning, too," he says, pointing to the foot-high veneer of rock that runs along the side of the basement wall. "That's real slow work. The stones are so heavy they can only lay a few at a time."

Inside, the drywall hanger holds a section of wallboard in place while his partner nails it to the studs.

The older man waves us over. Jerry walks up beside him and slaps him on the back. "I can't believe they got you working on a Saturday, Cecil. I didn't think you ever worked on a Saturday."

"You know how rich folks are," Cecil says. "Dr. A-rab thinks we can work twenty-four hours a day, long as he gets to move in when he wants to." Greenwood Construction, the outfit they all work for, is building this house for an Iraqi doctor who works at the new hospital on the other side of town. Jerry says none of the men can pronounce the doctor's name. Behind his back they call him Dr. A-rab. They don't call him anything to his face.

Jerry laughs, and I look at Ginny to see if she notices him just going along with the joke. Jerry never says things like this himself, but for all these men know, he thinks the same way they do. People around here will laugh at anything, even in this day and time. Last week, Jerry had a friend of his come over to watch the Wildcats play on TV. At halftime, they got to talking about how it's got so black people have it even better than white people, but are they satisfied? The man had his feet propped up on our coffee table and a bowl of popcorn on his lap. "Did I tell you what I heard about Martin Luther King Day?" he asked Jerry. "This is the first time we took it off at the plant, and the manager said, maybe if they kill four more of 'em, we can take off the whole damn week."

This is evidence that Jerry isn't good enough for my mother. Of course he isn't. This silence in the face of injustice is only one of the things I don't like about him.

I can't just be nice to people and act as if everything they do is all right with me. This semester in English we did a unit on the Holocaust. We read *Anne Frank: The Diary of a Young Girl* and saw a film after so the students who are too dumb or too lazy to read the book could pass the test. Sometimes, at night, the faces of people in the movie come back to me. Sometimes, looking at the pictures, you can't tell any difference between the women and the men, or even the rich from the poor.

The drywall man sets his foot on a bucket of Elmer's Spackle and lights a cigarette. He waves his hand, cigarette and all, toward my mother and me. "Which one of these good-looking women do you claim?" he asks.

Jerry hugs my mother around the waist. With his other arm, he reaches for me. His hand feels cold and dry against the back of my neck. "I'm a lucky man, Cecil. I claim 'em both."

We have just turned to leave when the doctor drives up the hill, steering his bright yellow SUV gently over the deep ruts in the road. He walks around the passenger side to help his wife out of the car. She stands, running long, white fingers through her short bright-red hair. She wears a waist-length suede jacket trimmed with light-colored fur. Creases as perfect as mitered corners run the length of her jeans.

The doctor gets his daughter out of the car seat and hands her to his wife. The little girl wears a jacket like her mother's and has a red ribbon tied around her long dark hair. When the woman sets the little girl on the ground, the child grabs her around the legs and presses her face against the back of her mother's knees, as though she is afraid her mother will get too far away. They remind me of a pair of stuffed polar bears Jerry bought me one year for Christmas. The baby hung onto its mother's neck with a pair of snaps sewn into its paws.

"He doesn't like the doctor much, does he?" I ask Jerry when we are in the car headed home. "The drywall man, I mean."

"Cecil likes him all right. Doc's not a bad guy. That's his second wife he had with him. George Green told me his first wife got killed in a plane crash."

Ginny pulls off her mittens and lays them on the dashboard. "Has he still got family in Iran?"

"I think his mother is still there. I asked him one time if he'd like to go back. He said he missed it sometimes, but this was his home now and he'd just have to make the best of it."

When I was little, while Ginny worked part time and studied accounting at a community college in Lexington, I lived with my grandparents. They rented a house from a man who'd grown tired of farming and sold almost all of his land to a developer, but still couldn't bring himself to let go of the family home.

In a shed out back, my grandfather repaired small appliances and refinished furniture. Most of it belonged to people he went to church with. He barely made enough to scrape by, but he said it was worth it if he didn't have to live in a city up north. He said all you could do in Cleveland, best as he could figure, was be poor and watch it snow.

At one time my grandmother took in sewing to help pay the bills, but when I lived with them she had fits of depression, when, for days, she couldn't do anything but sleep all the time with the shades closed. Even on her good days she would never chance opening the door to strangers, fearing bill collectors or women from the Sunshine Circle at the Baptist church down the road. "Libby," she'd say softly, whenever we heard a knock. "Libby. Go see who it is."

Usually it was someone to see my grandfather, and I'd send the caller out back to the shed. But if somebody caught us before my grandmother could get back to the bedroom and hide, she'd grab me roughly by the shoulders and we'd squat at the edge of the sofa, so low we didn't cast a single shadow against the bare white wall.

Every other weekend, Ginny came down. I'd stand at the window for hours ahead of time and watch for her rusty red Maverick to roll down the hill.

Sometimes she brought me chocolate candy, and once a Barbie doll dressed like Scarlet O'Hara in *Gone with the Wind*. I played with the doll while she was there, but as soon as she was gone, I took all its clothes off and lost it somewhere under the bed. Once I clung to her in the doorway and whimpered when she got ready to leave. I could smell the muskiness of her perfume, could feel the moist heat of her throat. But she unfastened my arms and pressed my palms together as though she meant to help me say a prayer.

"Don't start, Libby," she said, her voice steady and low. "If you start making it hard for me to leave, I'll have to quit coming at all."

Sometimes in secret, I cried myself to sleep, missing her. But from then on, I treated her like a visiting celebrity. If she took me on her lap to coax my head into the curve of her shoulder, or if she held my hand as I trotted along beside her in the cool grass of the yard, I stayed alert for the slightest loosening of her attention. Then, before she even realized she'd grown tired of me, I'd spring up and dash away.

My grandmother told me that Ginny almost got married a few months before she had me. A boy she knew in high school offered to make her an honest woman. Those were his exact words. He even bought her an engagement ring, not a diamond, of course, under the circumstances, but an ivory rosebud with tiny emeralds turned out at the sides like leaves.

The boy worked for a tool-and-die company thirty miles away in Richmond, but three or four times a week after work, he drove down. He and Ginny would sit in the driveway in his red Firebird, listening to a rock station on the ratio. An ugly boy with a thin neck and no knack for conversation, he kept his hands carefully in the curve of the steering wheel, as if to touch a girl in her condition might be a sin beyond all hope of grace.

It was the boy who decided it would be better if they got married quietly at the courthouse. But the day of the wedding, he came down with a stomach virus and stayed in Richmond, and somehow he never got around to asking again.

Jerry twists his head around when he hears Ginny and me coming through the kitchen door. He is propped up over the dinette table on his elbows, blueprints spread out in front of him.

"I got something to show you in a minute," he says, taking the bag of groceries from Ginny and setting it on the kitchen counter before he goes out to the car for the rest.

When we have everything in, Ginny stands behind him, leaning over his shoulder. He takes her arm and hangs it around his neck. He covers her hand with his. He always has to be touching her. Whenever they go anywhere, he tucks his index finger into one of the belt loops on her jeans. He follows a half step behind her, like a blind man.

"Look at this," he says, pausing to kiss the palm of her hand. "This could be our house."

Ginny pulls her arm loose and turns away. She begins to stack canned vegetables into the cabinet over the stove. "I've got this trailer paid for. Why do we need a house?"

Just as if he thinks she's still standing there, watching him, Jerry points out all the rooms. "Look here. There's a big bathroom off the master bedroom," he says. "And a utility room next to the kitchen. You always said how you wished I'd build on a little room where you could put in a washer and dryer."

I take a fudge bar out of the package and put the rest in the freezer. Then I sit down at the table, my left arm covering a close-up diagram of the trusses that go in the roof. "I'll bet a place like that would cost a lot."

But he ignores me to focus all his attention on my mother, who folds a paper sack into a small, neat square and doesn't turn around. "Come on, Ginny. At least look at it. I've already got a lot marked off at my grandpa's farm out on 39. He said he'd give me the deed whenever I got ready to build."

He takes a pencil out of his shirt pocket. With a ruler, he draws the floor plan onto clean sheets of paper to see how many ways he can find to move the rooms around. "I can do almost all of the work myself, at night and on the weekend. The lot's just like a down payment. I already called the bank to check."

Ginny tears open a bag of dry cat food and shakes some into the bowl by the door. "What's wrong with this place?" she asks, bending to scratch the cat behind its yellow ears. "It doesn't make sense to borrow all that money when you can just live here with me."

At the Laundromat, Ginny reads *Redbook* while I sort the clothes. When I've got all the washers going, I take the leftover quarters and buy us each a diet soda.

"Are you going to marry Jerry?" I ask, handing her the can.

She shrugs. "He wants us to get married. But I don't know. I kind of like things the way they are now."

"I'm never going to get married," I announce. "As soon as me and Gina graduate from high school, we're going to join the Peace Corps."

Ginny looks at me for a moment, as if she's sizing me up. "You just might. Funny you should say that. When we first met, that's what Stevie and I said we were going to do."

But of course I know this story already, how the night before my father left for boot camp, he and Ginny lay on the narrow bed in his one-room apartment, listening to a Blind Faith album on the radio. He held Ginny's face between his hands. "It's not like Vietnam," he said. "Now we've got all those smart bombs. I'll be back in no time. You'll see."

Ginny closes the magazine, drops it to the empty metal chair beside her, and looks across at the glass door, but it's late, the street is empty, and we have the place to ourselves. "Maybe I should just go on and marry him," she says. "It's not like it would change things all that much. Would it?"

Why is she asking me? "Maybe it's because of Stevie. Maybe you still think he might come back."

She tilts her chin up, and she smiles a little, as if somehow this has struck her as funny, but I can't tell whether she's laughing at me or at herself. "No." She goes to the dryer, opens the door, and reaches in to see if the clothes are dry. "I was absolutely crazy about your daddy. I thought he hung the moon. I almost told him about you, before he left, but I didn't. Did you know that? I could have told him. I know he liked me. Cared about me, even. But he didn't love me, Libby, not really. Young as I was, even I had sense enough to know that."

Saturday afternoon I lie on the couch with an afghan pulled up to my chin, reading a romance novel I keep losing interest in. *Maybe she should go ahead and marry him,* I think, watching Ginny pace back and forth between the mess of tax forms scattered across the kitchen table to the window where she stands watching, waiting for Jerry to get home. He's two hours late, and it isn't like him. I've watched her get more and more worried, wondering where he is.

She'll never admit worrying, of course. I know that, too, and I wonder if, for a different reason, she ever stood by the window this way waiting for my father, for Stevie, who not only didn't come back before she knew it, but didn't come back at all. I heard Jerry tell somebody once that Ginny reminded him of a stray from the dog pound. Hit a dog so often, he said, and no matter how hungry it is, it hangs back until it's sure what you've got in your hand.

I hear the car first, but she beats me to the door. "Finally," she says, leaning her forehead against the glass in the storm door, clouding it when she breathes.

She goes back to the table, and I go to the door to wait. But instead of coming inside, Jerry opens the car door and stands behind it, motioning for me. I crack the door and he yells, "Tell your mother to put some shoes on. I want to show her something."

"He wants you," I say, turning back to Ginny, and she's muttering, "I don't have time to fool with him right now," but she goes anyway to the closet and pulls on her shoes. I don't even bother with a jacket; I run out ahead of her in my socks.

Jerry has closed the car door and leans against the fender, grinning. I'm tiptoeing across the gravel to keep it from hurting my feet. "Go get your shoes," he says. "We're going for a ride." And I do.

I beat Ginny back outside, and Jerry is still in the same silly mood. When he sees me, he sweeps off his Greenwood Construction cap and bows low. "Your chariot waits," he says, flipping the front seat forward to let me crawl in the back.

"Where are we going?" Ginny asks, walking to the passenger side of the car and zipping up her blue parka with gloveless fingers.

Jerry lays his hand on her back, pushing her gently toward the car. "Don't ask so many questions. Just come on."

"Can't you even tell me where we're going?" But she yields to the weight of his hand.

On the road, it seems like we drive for miles. Every time Ginny opens her mouth to ask questions, Jerry grins and turns the radio up louder to keep from answering. By the time we're on the main road, he's singing along with Bruce Springsteen at the top of his lungs.

We pass the Iranian doctor's house, the yard recently planted with shrubs and trees. A few miles more, and Jerry turns onto a gravel road. We cross a narrow bridge and pass a white farmhouse, following a road that seems to be leading us straight into the wilderness. He twists the knob to turn the music down. "Be patient," he says. "It's not far now." But Ginny has her head leaned back against the seat, looking out the window and not saying anything, as though she is resigned to be going along with him on this ride.

Maybe a mile and a half more, and Jerry pulls onto the shoulder of the road and climbs out. He closes the door and walks down the lane in front of us. Then, he turns to look behind him, stretching out his hand to my mother.

At the end of the road, the woods open onto a rolling meadow framed by a row of low hills. "Is this—?" Ginny says, and he nods, patting her arm.

"Wait here. I've got to get something from the car."

We stand shivering, listening to the trunk open and close, and in a few moments he is back, carrying a hammer and some wooden stakes. He throws them on the ground beside my feet and then reels blue flagging from the pocket of his jacket the way a magician, out of nowhere, produces scarves.

He's been grinning ever since we left the house, but for a second he looks uncertain, watching Ginny's face. "Well? Where do you want me to put the house?"

She hesitates, but when she starts to speak, he interrupts her.

"I've got a deed to thirty acres of ground that run from the creek to the crest of that hill over there. But here's the deal. It's not recorded yet, but I had Grandpa deed it to both of us. I've got the deed in the glove compartment if you want to see."

"It's your family land, Jerry. You shouldn't—"

"That's what Grandpa said. But I told him to trust me, and I don't know why, but he did."

It's crazy, that's what the look on her face says, but he shows her how the house might look facing south, with a wide front porch and some flowers growing by the porch steps.

A faint outline in the silvery sky, the new moon is tipped back, resting on its heel above the white branches of a sycamore that stands beside the creek. The wind catches Ginny's hair and blows it back, and with his index finger Jerry traces the outlines of the house in the air, and she nods, seeing it in her mind.

"It would be pretty," she says, finally. "Still. You should have asked me first." But though she's never willing to give in without a protest, I can tell she's only making a point for future reference, the decision is already made.

"It's for Christmas," Jerry says. I can't see his face, but his voice sounds light as though he is smiling, as though he knows Ginny as well as I do. "If I had asked you first, it would have ruined my big surprise."

He steps behind her, his chin across the top of her head, his arms around her waist. She rests against him, sliding her cold hands into his sleeves.

"That's the best place, where you're looking. We'll leave the poplar tree and that stand of sugar maples. It's good and level, too, won't take much grade work. In the summer, we'll have shade."

"What do you think, Libby?" he asks, suddenly, looking around for me. Clouds scoot by in the sky above us, and the wind picks up, kicking up leaves and bending the treetops toward the west. I'm freezing, and seeing me shiver, he steps a little away from Ginny and reaches out a hand to drag me in.

We stand together, watching the moon grow bright, and I think maybe even I can see a house there, if I try hard, with its yellow windows glowing against the falling dark. After a while, with my left hand tucked into Jerry's jacket pocket and my body sheltered between my mother and him, maybe, for a little while anyway, I can forget about the cold.

About the Author

Wanda Fries is a poet and fiction writer who lives in Somerset with her husband Denny, a geologist. They have two grown children, Jesse and Megan. Her books include two novels, *Ash Grove* and *In the Absence of Angels,* and a book of poetry *Cassandra among the Greeks.*

She has won numerous awards for her work, including the Al Smith Fellowship from the Kentucky Council of the Arts and the Cornelia Dozer Cooper grant.

She is currently at work on a novel about Catherine Blake, wife of the visionary Romantic poet, artist, and printer, William. Her primary research for this novel (in England and Edinburgh, Scotland) received funding through a grant from the Kentucky Foundation for Women.

www.ingramcontent.com/pod-product-compliance
Lightning Source LLC
Chambersburg PA
CBHW021933170626
46807CB00007B/3081